His gaze didn't budge from Kate. She was embarrassed.

"Oh, I have no one to blame. I did it to myself," she said wistfully.

"I may not be an expert on babies, but I do know how they're made. And I'm fairly certain there has to be a partner." It was his turn to shoot her a confused look.

"Adoption," she said.

And then he gave her another.

"Surely you've heard of adopting a baby before," she said with an exasperated look.

"Of course I have. I just didn't know that was your circumstance," he said stupidly.

Looking closer at the baby, Dallas couldn't help but notice the boy had dark curly hair.

Not unlike his own.

STOCKYARD SNATCHING

USA TODAY Bestselling Author

BARB HAN

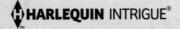

My deepest thanks to Allison Lyons. It's hard to believe this is already
our 10th book together! Working with you is a dream come true
and I'm so very grateful. Special nod to Jill Marsal for your unwavering
support and guidance (and brilliance!).

My love to Brandon, Jacob and Tori. I'm so proud of each one of you.
You're bright, talented and have the best quirks!

To Amelia Rae, you stole our hearts a year ago. Happy 1st Birthday!

And to you, Babe. I can't even imagine being on this journey without you.
All my love. All my life.

Recycling programs
for this product may
not exist in your area.

ISBN-13: 978-0-373-69922-3

Stockyard Snatching

Copyright © 2016 by Barb Han

Printed in U.S.A.

HARLEQUIN®
www.Harlequin.com

USA TODAY bestselling author **Barb Han** lives in north Texas with her very own hero-worthy husband, three beautiful children, a spunky golden retriever/standard poodle mix and too many books in her to-read pile. In her downtime, she plays video games and spends much of her time on or around a basketball court. She loves interacting with readers and is grateful for their support. You can reach her at barbhan.com.

Books by Barb Han

Harlequin Intrigue

Cattlemen Crime Club

Stockyard Snatching

Mason Ridge

Texas Prey
Texas Takedown
Texas Hunt
Texan's Baby

The Campbells of Creek Bend

Witness Protection
Gut Instinct
Hard Target

Rancher Rescue

Harlequin Intrigue Noir

Atomic Beauty

CAST OF CHARACTERS

Kate Williams—Adopting a baby from Safe Haven Adoption Agency and moving to Bluff, Texas, was supposed to give her a new lease on life. An attempted kidnapping and news that other babies adopted from the agency are being abducted have her reassessing whom she can trust.

Dallas O'Brien—He inherited the family's successful cattle ranch with five of his brothers following their parents' deaths. After amassing his own fortune, he had a brief relationship that could have produced a child. The question is...could Dallas be the father of Kate's adopted baby?

Susan Hanover—She claims to have had Dallas's baby and then she disappeared without a trace. Her last-known trail leads to Safe Haven Adoption Agency.

Wayne Morton—This private investigator (hired by Dallas) is killed while following up on a lead with Safe Haven Adoption Agency.

Tommy Johnson—The sheriff who grew up at the O'Brien ranch and considers them family.

Allen Lentz—He's the second in command at the charity run by Kate. Does his interest in her run purely professional? If not, how far will he go to make it personal?

Raphael Manuel—This criminal might be linked to Susan.

William Seaver—The lawyer who handled Kate's adoption...and Susan's.

Harold Matthews—He handles much of the paperwork at Safe Haven Adoption Agency, but does he do more than that?

Chapter One

It was a bitterly cold early October morning. The temperature gauge on Dallas O'Brien's dashboard read 17 degrees, beneath a gray sky thick with clouds.

As it turned out, the Lone Star State had a temper and its tantrums came in the form of cold snaps that made him miss having a winter beard. Dallas hated cold.

Yesterday, the sun had been out and he had been in short sleeves. Texas weather—like life—could turn on a dime.

Another frigid breeze blasted through Dallas, piercing his coat as he slid out of the driver's seat and then closed the door of his pickup. He flipped up the corners of his collar. Since there was no traffic, he'd made it to the supply store in record time. Normally the place would be open, but Jessie had been running late ever since his wife gave birth to twins early last month.

A car tooled around the back of the building and across the parking lot. Was that Kate Williams, the proud owner of the soup kitchen, The Food Project? Dallas hadn't had a chance to meet her yet, with everything going on at the ranch after his parents' deaths.

A female came out of the driver's side, rounded the car and moved to the rear passenger door. From this distance, Dallas estimated she wasn't an inch more than five and a half feet tall. He couldn't see much of her figure through her thick, buttoned-to-the-collar, navy blue peacoat. Her cable-knit scarf looked more like an afghan wrapped around her neck. He suppressed a laugh. Apparently, she didn't do cold any better than Dallas.

From what little he could see of her legs, she had on blue jeans. Furry brown boots rose above her calves. She wore expensive clothing for someone who owned a soup kitchen. And apparently—Dallas glanced at his watch—that process began at five thirty in the morning.

This had to be her, he reasoned, as she pulled a baby out of the backseat, bundled from head to toe in what looked like a fitted blue quilt. Blue.

A boy?

Didn't that twist up Dallas's insides?

First, his ex Susan Hanover had dropped the bomb that he was going to be a father. Then she'd pulled a disappearing act. And even the best private investigator money could buy hadn't been able to locate her or the baby since.

Knowing Susan, she'd been lying to trap him into a wedding ring. Dallas's finger itched thinking about it.

With her and the baby gone, all he had left were

questions—questions that kept him tossing and turning most nights.

What if she'd been lying? What if she hadn't? What if Dallas had a child out there somewhere? What if his child needed him?

Dallas would never be able to rest until he had answers.

Walking away from a child wasn't something an O'Brien could ever do. Dallas had already lost his parents, and family meant everything to him.

As Ms. Williams closed the door to her vehicle, shivering in the cold, a male figure emerged from around the side of her building. The guy had on a hoodie and his face was angled toward the ground. His clothes were dirty, dark and layered. He was either homeless or trying to look the part.

The guy glanced around nervously as he approached Ms. Williams.

Didn't that get Dallas's radar jacked up to full alert? He strained to get a better view. *Come on. Look up.*

All this guy would have to do would be ask Ms. Williams a question to distract her—say, what time the place opened. She would answer; he would rob her and then run. There were plenty of places to disappear downtown or in the neighborhood near the stockyard.

It would be a perfect crime, because not only was she holding a baby, but her thick clothing would weigh her down, making it impossible for her to catch him.

Well, a perfect crime if Dallas wasn't right there watching.

Then again, this really could be a man in need of

a meal. Experience had taught Dallas not to jump the gun when it came to people. There was no shortage of homeless, even in a small town like Bluff, Texas.

The times he had driven by this location early in the morning and found the line of needy individuals stretched around the block were too many to count. He was pretty certain Ms. Williams's neighbors on Main Street didn't appreciate her clientele. None of them would be wandering through the stores after a meal to buy handmade jewelry or quaint Texas souvenirs. These businesses were important to the local economy.

Just then, the hooded figure lifted his head and made a grab for the baby.

This wasn't a robbery; it was a kidnapping.

Dallas spewed curse words as he ran full throttle toward them. "Stop right there!" he shouted.

Ms. Williams fought back and her attacker shifted position, ensuring she was between him and Dallas.

The baby cried, which seemed to agitate the attacker. Ms. Williams kicked the guy where no man wanted the tip of a boot. He coughed, then cursed as he seemed to catch sight of Dallas out of the corner of his eye.

The man shouted as he struggled to take the baby out of Ms. Williams's arms. "Don't come any closer!" His voice was agitated and Dallas didn't recognize it. Must not be someone local. The guy forced the woman back a few steps with him, a knife to her throat. "I didn't want to do it like this, but now she's coming with me."

The baby wailed and Dallas came to a stop.

This situation had gone sour in a heartbeat.

To make matters worse, all Dallas could see clearly

of Ms. Williams was a set of terrified blue eyes staring at him. She had that desperate-mother look that said she'd do anything to save her son. Dallas's heart squeezed as she held tight to her baby with the determination only a loving mom could possess.

He hoped like hell she wouldn't do anything stupid.

Tires squealed from behind the building and Dallas instantly wished it would be his best friend, Sheriff Tommy Johnson. No way would Tommy be dumb enough to come roaring up, however. His friend was smarter than that and a better lawman.

A vehicle rounded the corner and lurched to a stop nearby. The white minivan's sliding door opened.

The attacker broke eye contact to look. If Dallas had a shot at taking the guy down, he'd grab it.

"Toss your keys to me," the kidnapper shouted to him.

Dallas dug a set from his pocket and pitched them forward.

If he didn't make a move soon, this jerk would disappear into that van with mother and baby. She'd most likely be killed and her body dumped before they left the county. Dallas had read about vicious illegal adoption rings in the area and stories of mothers being killed for their infants.

Between the hoodie pulled over the thug's forehead and the turtleneck covering his jaw, Dallas couldn't get a good look at his face. The guy glanced away again, as if calculating the odds of getting inside the vehicle before Dallas could catch him. Then he bent to grab the keys.

It was now or never.

Dallas lunged toward his target and knocked the guy's arm away from Kate's throat. The sheer amount of fabric she had wrapped around her neck made certain the blade wouldn't get anywhere near her skin. For the first time in his life, Dallas thanked the cold weather.

Breaking free, Ms. Williams bolted toward her car, while trying to soothe the crying infant.

In the bustle, the attacker broke out of Dallas's grip and darted toward the vehicle. Damn. No plates.

"The sheriff is on his way," Dallas said in desperation, knowing full well his target was about to hop into that van and disappear.

Just as expected, the guy hurled himself in the open door and, without waiting for it to close, shouted at the driver to go. On cue, the van swerved, then sped away.

Dallas muttered a curse. Pulling out his cell, he told Ms. Williams to stay put. Even though his pickup wasn't far, he couldn't leave her to give chase. No way would he risk this guy circling back or sending others to finish the job. Dallas would have to stay with her to ensure her safety.

At least this morning wasn't a total bust. The baby was safe in his mother's arms. Dallas could call his friend the sheriff, who would track down the minivan while Dallas guarded Ms. Williams.

"Where are you?" he asked as soon as Tommy picked up.

"A couple of blocks from Main Street," the lawman replied. "Why? You okay?"

"I'm in the back parking lot of the soup kitchen and a man just tried to abduct Ms. Williams's baby. There's a white Mazda minivan heading in your direction. He hopped inside it before I could get to him. No tags in front," Dallas reported, noticing for the first time that he was practically panting from adrenaline. He took a deep breath and then finished relaying the details of what had just gone down.

"Is there a high point you can get to for a visual on the minivan?" Tommy asked.

Dallas kept an eye on Ms. Williams as he climbed on top of the closed Dumpster to see if he could spot the vehicle. She had managed to settle the baby. Dallas was certain her hands would be shaking from her own adrenaline, and he was grateful for the few extra minutes he'd get while she fumbled with securing her son in the car seat. The panicked look on her face said she'd get as far away as possible the second she could.

"No. I don't see him," Dallas said.

"I'm on Main now. A couple of blocks from your location, but I don't see anyone on the street." Tommy asked Dallas to stand by while he gave his deputies a description of the vehicle. "I'm sending someone over to you just in case the guy is on his way back or sends someone else."

"Call me back when you know anything. I have to check on Ms. Williams and make sure she doesn't do anything stupid," Dallas said, knowing full well that her eyes would haunt him if he didn't ensure she was okay. It would be a long time before he shook off the image of those frightened sky blues, and he had to admit to being a little interested to see what the rest of her face looked like. He told himself it was protective instinct mixed with curiosity and nothing more.

Besides, she'd been as blindsided by all this as he had. He hopped down and jogged toward her sedan. "Ma'am."

She spun around with a gasp. "Kate. It's Kate."

He brought his hand up, palm out, to help communicate the idea that he wasn't there to hurt her.

"I'm Dallas O'Brien." He offered a handshake. She was most likely still in shock, and from the look of her wild eyes, she was in full get-the-heck-out-of-Dodge mode. "The sheriff is sending someone over to talk to us."

She stood there, frozen, for several seconds, as if her mind might be clicking through options. She didn't seem to realize there was only one: talk to Dallas.

"Do you know who that was?" he asked, figuring he already knew the answer. But he wanted to get her talking.

"No. I've never seen him before in my life." Her breath was visible in the cold air as she spoke, and even though she had on a thick layer of clothes, she was shivering. That, too, was most likely caused by residual adrenaline.

"First of all, I want to make sure you and your baby are safe. Can we go inside the building?" Dallas's own adrenaline surge was wearing off and he was starting to feel the biting wind again. He'd stay with her until law enforcement arrived and then he'd get supplies and head back to the ranch.

"Okay. Yes. Sure. I was going in anyway before—" She stopped midsentence, as if she couldn't bring herself to finish.

Then another round of panic seemed to set in.

"No. Never mind. We have to go somewhere else," she insisted, her gaze darting from left to right.

"He's gone. They won't be back, especially not while I'm here," Dallas stated.

"You can't know that for certain," she said quickly.

"Kate, I can assure you—"

"No. You can't. We can talk, but we have to do it somewhere else." She glanced about, her terror and desperation mounting.

Dallas's cell phone buzzed. He fished it from his coat pocket and checked the screen. "This call is from the sheriff. I need to answer."

She nodded.

"Give me some good news," Dallas said into the phone.

"Wish I could. Seems your white Mazda minivan is just as slippery as your suspect. There's no sign of either anywhere. We have no plans to give up searching. You'll be the first to know when we locate him," Tommy said with a frustrated sigh.

Dallas thanked his friend for the update and then ended the call, cursing under his breath.

An expectant victim stared at him, needing reassurance.

He shook his head.

"I have to get out of here before they come back,"

she said, making a move toward the driver's side of her sedan.

"Hold on," Dallas cautioned. "What makes you so sure he'll try again?"

Chapter Two

"I feel too exposed here. Can we go somewhere be-sides my soup kitchen? I need to get away from this place," Kate blurted out. It was then she realized that she'd been holding her breath. She exhaled, trying to calm her rapid pulse.

"A deputy is on his way," the handsome cowboy said, and his name finally sank in. Dallas O'Brien. She knew that name from somewhere. But where?

Her mind raced. She was still shocked that anyone would try to rip her baby from her arms in the mid-dle of town. She'd waited so long for him, had been through hell and back. What kind of horrible person would try to take him away?

Tears threatened, but Kate forced herself to hold them at bay.

"My son will need to eat soon and I'd rather not feed him in the parking lot, whether a deputy is com-ing or not," she said, glancing from Dallas to Jackson.

The cowboy looked around and then checked his watch. "Fine. We're going to the sheriff's office to give statements, then," he said.

Jackson would be safe there, so she nodded.

"I don't have a child safety seat in my truck, so we'll have to take your car," he added, his voice sturdy as steel.

As calming as his presence was, her body still shook from fear of that man coming back and the horror of him trying to pry Jackson out of her arms.

"You gave him your keys," she reminded Dallas, wasting no time slipping into the driver's seat, while he took the passenger side of her sedan.

"Those? That'll get him into my old post office box," he said with a wry grin. It was the first time she really noticed Dallas's good looks. He had a strong, square jaw and intelligent dark eyes.

"I'd like to go home," Kate said as she turned the ignition. "Can the deputy meet us there?"

"Too risky," Dallas said.

It took a second for her to realize that he meant the men might know where she lived.

Could they?

Being single and living alone, she'd taken great pains to ensure her personal information remained private. Then again, with the internet these days, it seemed there was no real privacy left, and most people in the small town knew each other anyway. All a determined bad guy would have to do was ask around and he'd be able to figure out where she lived.

"All of Jackson's supplies are there, except what's inside the diaper bag in the backseat," she said as she pulled onto Main from the alley.

Dallas surveyed the area and she realized that with

her driving, he would be able to keep watch for the minivan in case it returned. She racked her brain, trying to figure out how she knew him.

"We can pick up new diapers if need be. I don't want to go to your place until we know it's safe. For now, take a right at the next stoplight," Dallas said. He sent a text and she assumed he was telling the sheriff about their change in plans.

Normally, being told what to do was like fingernails on a chalkboard to Kate. In this case, she decided it was better to do as Dallas said. At least he was strong and capable. She already knew he could handle himself in a fight, and he had just saved her and Jackson, so she knew she could trust him.

"Three blocks ahead, take another right, then a left at the stop sign," he instructed.

She did. The horror of what had just happened was finally sinking in and it dawned on her how lucky she'd been that someone was there to help.

"I owe you an apology for being rude to you. Thank you for stepping in to save my son," she said. "You didn't have to get involved."

"You're welcome," Dallas replied. "I'm just glad I was there to help. I don't normally go to the supply store on Wednesdays."

"Your change of plans probably just saved Jackson's life." She shivered at the thought of what might've happened if this cowboy hadn't been there to intervene. "I know it saved mine."

Reality was setting in, which also made her realize there was no one to open the kitchen this morning.

She needed to call her assistant director or dozens of people would go hungry.

"I have to make sure the kitchen opens on time. Is it okay if I make a quick call before we go inside?" She parked in the lot of the sheriff's office and gripped the steering wheel. "A lot of people are counting on me for a meal."

Dallas nodded, while staring at the screen of his cell. "Make an excuse as to why you can't do it yourself, and put the call on speaker. I don't want you to give away what happened yet. Got it?"

She shot him a sideways glance. "Why?"

"That was a planned attack. Those men knew exactly when and where you'd be alone. The sheriff will want to know if someone close to you gave them that information, and we have to assume it could've been anyone, even people you trust."

An icy chill ran down her spine. "You think one of my employees might've supplied that?" she asked, not bothering to mask her shock. Who would want to hurt Jackson or her? He was just a baby. Her mind could scarcely wrap around the fact that someone had tried to take him in the first place. Panic flooded her at the memory. "Who would plan something like this?"

"The sheriff will help find the answer to that question," Dallas said, his voice a study in composure, whereas she was falling apart.

"None of this seems real," she said, bile rising, burning her throat. "I think I might be sick."

"Take a few deep breaths." His voice was like calm, soothing water pouring over her.

She did as he suggested.

"Better?" he asked.

"Yes." She apologized again.

"Don't be sorry for wanting to protect your child," Dallas said. And there was an underlying note in his tone she couldn't easily identify. Was he a father?

"You have every right to be upset," he said.

"It's just that I moved here for a safe environment." And now it felt as if everything in her life was unraveling. Again.

"Who are you going to call to open the kitchen?" Dallas asked.

Oh, right. She'd gotten distracted once more. Her mind was spinning in a thousand directions. "Allen Lentz. He's my second in command and my right hand."

Her phone weighed almost nothing and yet shook as she held it. She paused. "You don't think…?"

"Get him on speaker." There was a low rumble to Dallas O'Brien's voice now, a deep baritone that sent a different kind of shiver racing down her spine— one that was unwelcome and inappropriate given the circumstances.

Her rescuer's name seemed so familiar and she couldn't figure out why. Wait a minute. Didn't his family own the Cattlemen Crime Club? She'd received an invitation to a Halloween Bash in a few weeks, which was a charity fund-raiser, and realized that she'd seen his family name on the invite.

In fact, her kitchen was one of the beneficiaries of his family's generosity. She hadn't met any of the

O'Briens yet. She'd read that they'd lost their parents in an accident a few weeks ago.

So far, she'd dealt with office staff, even though she'd been told that the O'Briens personally visited every one of the charities they supported.

She hadn't expected Dallas O'Brien to be this intense, down-to-earth or staggeringly handsome. Not that she could think of a good reason why not. Maybe since he'd grown up with money she'd expected someone entitled or spoiled.

And yet now wasn't the time to think about how off her perception had been or that her pulse kicked up a few notches when he was close. She chalked her adrenaline rush up to the morning's events and closed the door on that topic.

Lack of sleep was beginning to distort her brain. No one had prepared her for the fact that she'd worry so much or rest so little once the baby arrived. No way would she admit defeat to her parents, either. They'd been clear about how much disdain they had for her decision to have a baby alone. Her mother had been mortified when she found out Kate was getting a divorce, so adopting a baby by herself was right up there on the list of ways she'd let her mother down.

Kate had expected her mom to come around once she met Jackson, but was still waiting for that day to happen.

This battle was hers to fight alone.

And none of that mattered when she held her little guy in her arms. No matter how tired she might be or how distanced she was from her family, she wouldn't trade the world for the baby of her heart.

"Hey, what's going on?" Allen asked, sounding surprisingly alert for five fifty in the morning. The phone must've startled him.

"I need your help. Can you open the kitchen for me?" she asked, trying to think up a reasonable excuse to sell him. Then she went with the tried-and-true. "Jackson kept me up all night again."

"Oh, poor baby. And I'm talking about you," Allen said with a laugh. He yawned, and she heard the sound clearly through the phone. "His days and nights still confused?"

"Yes, and I have the bags under my eyes to prove it," she said, hating that she had to lie to cover what had really happened. Allen had been nothing but a good employee and friend, and she hated deception.

"No problem. I'll throw on some clothes and head over," he said.

"You're a lifesaver, Allen."

"Don't I know it," he quipped. There was a rustling noise as if he was tossing off his covers and getting out of bed.

"I'll owe you big-time for this one," Kate said.

"Good. Then get a babysitter for Friday night and let me take you out to dinner." He didn't miss a beat.

Out of the corner of her eye, Kate saw Dallas's jaw muscle clench. She couldn't tell if his reaction was good or bad.

"I don't know if I'll be in today," Kate said awkwardly. She quickly glanced at Dallas, realizing that she needed to redirect the conversation with Allen. "The Patsy family's donation should hit the bank today. Would you mind watching for it and letting me know when it arrives?"

"Got it," he said. "And don't think I didn't notice that you changed the subject."

"We've already gone over this, Allen. He's too little to leave with a sitter," Kate said quietly into the phone. Her cheeks heated as she talked about her lack of a life in front of a complete stranger, and especially one as good-looking as Dallas.

"That excuse doesn't fly with me and you know it," Allen said flatly.

Kate had no response.

"Fine. At least take me as your date to the Hackney party next weekend," he offered.

"I'm skipping that one, too. Can we talk about it later? I'm too tired to think beyond today," she said, then managed to end the call without any more embarrassing revelations about her life. The truth was her perspective had changed the instant Jackson had been placed in her arms. There was no man worth leaving her baby for, even for a night.

"Is he usually so…friendly?" Dallas asked.

"I stay out of my employees' personal lives," she said, hating the suspicion in Dallas's voice. "There's no way Allen would do anything to hurt me or Jackson."

"I take it there's no Mr. Williams to notify?" Dallas asked.

Clearly, he'd picked up on the fact that she was single. She'd listened intently for condemnation in his tone and was surprised she didn't find a hint. She'd expected to and more after cashing out her interests in the tech company she and her brother had started together and moving to a small town. If her own family couldn't get behind her choices, how could strangers?

"No. There isn't. Is that a problem?" she asked a little too sharply. Missing sleep didn't bring out the best in her, and she'd been only half lying about not sleeping last night due to Jackson's schedule or lack thereof. At his age, he took a bottle every four hours, day and night.

"Not for me personally. The sheriff will want to know, and I'm taking notes to speed along the process once we go inside." Dallas motioned toward the small notepad he'd taken out of his pocket.

"Oh. Right." As soon as Jackson was old enough to take care of himself—like, age eighteen—Kate planned to stay in bed an entire weekend. Maybe then she'd think clearly again. Heck, give her a hotel and room service and she'd stay there a whole week.

"Where's the father?" Dallas asked, still with no hint of disapproval in his voice.

"Out of the picture."

There was a beat of silence. "Ready to go inside and talk?" he asked at last, his brow arched.

"Yes. I'll just get Jackson from the backseat," she said defensively. There was no reason to be on guard, she reminded herself. Besides, what would she care if a stranger judged her?

Dallas stood next to her, holding the car door open. She thanked him as she pulled Jackson close to her chest. Just the thought of anything happening to her son...

She couldn't even go there.

"Can I help with the diaper bag?" Dallas held out his hand, still no hint of condemnation in his tone.

"You must have children." Kate managed to ease it off her shoulder without disturbing the baby, who was thankfully asleep again. Her nerves were settling down enough for her hands to finally stop shaking.

"Not me," he said, sounding a little defensive. What was that all about?

Kate figured the man's family status was none of her business. She was just grateful that Jackson was still asleep.

Thank the stars for car rides. They were the only way she could get her son down for a nap some days. It probably didn't hurt that he'd been awake most of the night. He'd been born with his days and nights mixed up.

Family man or not, Kate's life would be very different right now if Dallas hadn't been there. Tears threatened to release along with all the emotions she'd been holding in.

Or maybe it was the fact that she felt safe with Dallas, which was a curious thought given that he was a stranger.

This wasn't the time or place to worry about either. Kate needed to pull on all the strength she had for Jackson. He needed his mother to keep it together.

"I can't thank you enough," she said, knowing that she wouldn't be holding her baby right now if not for this man. "Not just for carrying a diaper bag, but for everything you did for us this morning."

Dallas nodded. He was tall, easily more than six foot. Maybe six foot two? He had enough muscles for her to know he put in serious time at the gym or on the ranch owned by him and his family. His hair was blacker than the sky on any clear night she'd seen. There was an intensity to him, too, and she had no doubt the man was good at whatever he put his mind to.

She told herself that the only reason she noticed was because they'd been in danger and he'd just saved her son's life.

DALLAS WALKED KATE into the sheriff's office and instructed her to take a seat anywhere she'd be comfortable.

Looking at the baby stirred up all kinds of feelings in him that he wasn't ready to deal with. Not until he knew for sure one way or the other about his own parenthood status. Being in limbo was the absolute worst feeling, apart from knowing that he was in no way ready to be a father.

And yet a part of him wondered what it would be like to have a little rug rat running around the ranch. He chalked the feeling up to missing his parents. Losing them so unexpectedly had delivered a blow to the family and left a hole that couldn't be filled. And then there was Dallas's guilt over not being available to help them out when they'd called. He'd been halfway to New Mexico with an unexpected problem in one of his warehouses.

His gut twisted as he thought about it. If he'd turned around his truck and come back like they'd asked, they'd still be alive.

Dallas needed to redirect his thoughts or his guilt would consume him again. An update from his private investigator, Wayne Morton, was overdue. When Morton had last made contact, three days ago, he'd believed he was on a trail that might lead to Susan's whereabouts. He'd been plenty busy at the ranch, trying to get his arms around the family business.

"Can I get anything for you or the baby?" Dallas asked Kate, needing a strong cup of coffee.

"Something warm would be nice," she said, wedging the sleeping baby safely in a chair.

Dallas nodded before making his exit as she began peeling off her scarf and layers of outerwear.

A few minutes later he returned with two steaming cups of brew. He hesitated at the door once he got a good look at her, and his pulse thumped. Calling her five and a half feet tall earlier had been generous. The only reason she seemed that height was the heeled boots she wore. Without them, she'd be five foot three at the most. She had on fitted jeans that hugged her curves and a deep blue sweater that highlighted her eyes— eyes that would challenge even the perfect blue sky of a gorgeous spring day. Her shiny blond hair was pulled off her face into a ponytail.

"Wasn't sure how you took yours, so I brought cream and sugar," he said, setting both cups on the side table near where she stood. He emptied his coat pocket of cream and sugar packets, ignoring his rapid heartbeat.

She thanked him before mixing the condiments into her cup.

The baby moved as she sat down next to him and she immediately scooped him up and brought him to her chest.

The infant wound up for a good cry, unleashed one, and Kate's stress levels appeared to hit the roof.

"He's got a healthy set of lungs," Dallas offered, trying to ease her tension.

"He's probably hungry. Is there a place where I can warm a bottle?" she asked, distress written in the wrinkle across her forehead.

Abigail, Tommy's secretary, appeared in the doorway before Dallas could answer. She'd been with the sheriff's office long before Tommy arrived and had become invaluable to him in the five years since he'd taken the job. She threatened to retire every year, and every year he made an offer she couldn't refuse.

"I can take care of that for you," she said. "Where's the bottle?"

"In there," Kate said, attempting to handle the baby and make a move for the diaper bag next to her. She couldn't quite manage it and started to tear up as Abigail shooed her away, scooping the bag off the floor.

"Thank you," Kate said, glancing from Abigail to Dallas.

"Don't be silly." The older woman just smiled. "You've been through a lot this morning." She motioned toward Jackson. "It'll get easier with him. The first few months are always the most difficult with a new baby."

Dallas felt as out of place in the conversation as catfish bait in a tilapia pond. And then a thought struck him. If he was a father—and he wasn't anywhere near ready to admit to the possibility just yet—he'd need to learn about diaper bags and 3:00 a.m. feedings. Kate's employee had taken her up-all-night excuse far too easily, which meant it happened enough for her to be able to know using it wouldn't be questioned.

Speaking of which, Allen seemed to know way too much about Kate's personal life, which could mean that the office employees were close, and it was clear he wanted more than a professional relationship with her. The guy was a little too cozy with his boss and Dallas didn't like it. She obviously refused his advances. A thought struck. Could that be enough for him to want to punish her by removing the only obstacle between them—her child?

He was probably reaching for a simple explanation. Even so, it was a question Dallas intended to bounce around with Tommy.

Dallas made a mental note to ask Kate more about her relationship with Allen as soon as the baby was calm again, which happened a few seconds after Abigail returned with a warmed bottle and he began feeding.

The look of panic didn't leave Kate's face entirely during the baby's meal, but she gazed lovingly at her son.

Dallas had questions and needed answers, the quicker the better. However, it didn't feel right interrupting mother and son during what looked to be a bonding moment.

But then, not being a father himself, what the hell did he know about it?

Sipping his coffee, he waited for Kate to speak first. It didn't take long. Another few minutes and she finally said, "I want to apologize about my behavior this morning. I'm not normally so…frazzled."

"You're doing better than you think," he said, offering reassurance.

"Am I?" she asked. "Because I feel like I'm all over the place emotionally."

"Trust me. You're doing fine."

Her shoulders relaxed a little and that made Dallas smile.

"I do have a question for you, though," he said.

She nodded.

"How well do you know your employees?" he asked, ignoring the most probable reason Allen's attraction grated on him so much. Dallas liked her, too.

"Some more than others, I guess." She shrugged. "We're a small office, so we talk."

The baby finished his bottle and she placed a cloth napkin over her shoulder before laying him across it and patting his back.

"What does that do?" Dallas's curiosity about babies was getting the best of him. His stress was also growing with every passing day that Morton didn't return his texts.

"Gets the gas out of his stomach. Believe me, you

want it out. If you don't he can cramp up and become miserable." She frowned.

"And when he's miserable, you're miserable."

"Exactly," she said, her tone wistful. A tear escaped, rolling down her cheek. She wiped it away and quickly apologized. "This whole parenting thing has been much harder than I expected."

"Whoever did this to you and left should be castrated," Dallas said. And he figured he was a hypocrite with that coming out of his mouth, given that he might have done the same to another woman. However, he had very strong feelings about the kind of man who didn't mind making a baby, but couldn't be bothered to stick around to be a father to the child. The operative word in his situation was that he might have *unwittingly* done that to someone. And he had no proof that Susan had actually been pregnant with his child, given that she'd disappeared when he'd offered to bring up the baby separately, instead of agreeing to her suggestion that they immediately marry. Her call had come out of the blue, months after they'd parted ways.

His gaze didn't budge from Kate. He expected some kind of reaction from her. All he saw was genuine embarrassment.

"Oh, I have no one to blame. I did it to myself," she said.

"I may not be an expert on babies, but I do know how they're made. And I'm fairly certain there has to be a partner." It was Dallas's turn to shoot her a confused look.

"Adoption," she said.

He gave her another.

"Surely you've heard of adopting a baby?" she asked tartly.

"Of course I have. I just didn't know that was your circumstance," he said stupidly.

Looking closer at the baby, Dallas couldn't help but notice the boy had dark curly hair.

Not unlike his own.

Chapter Three

Kate recognized the sheriff as soon as he stepped inside his office. Not only had she seen him around town, he'd stopped by the kitchen to welcome her when she'd first opened her doors.

He was close to Dallas O'Brien's height, so at least six feet tall. His hair was light brown and his eyes matched the shade almost perfectly.

She was relieved for the interruption, after sharing the news about Jackson being adopted, and especially after Dallas's reaction, which made no sense to her. He seemed fine with her being a single parent, but lost his ability to speak once she'd mentioned the adoption. What was up with that?

The sheriff acknowledged Dallas first and then offered a handshake to Kate.

Dallas relayed the morning's events succinctly and Kate's heart squeezed at hearing the words, knowing how close she'd been to losing her son. She reminded herself that she had Dallas to thank for thwarting the kidnapping attempt.

If he hadn't been there...

She shivered, deflecting the chill gripping her spine.

"Most kidnappings involve family. Sounds like that isn't the case here," the sheriff said. "We can't rule out the birth parents. What's your relationship with them?"

"None," Kate responded. She hadn't thought about the possibility that Jackson's biological parents could've changed their minds. "The adoption was closed, records sealed, based on the mother's request."

"I'll make contact with the agency to see if I can get any additional information from them. I wouldn't count on it without a court order, though," Tommy warned. "What's the name?"

"Safe Haven," she stated.

Tommy nodded. "Good. I know who they are."

Kate held tighter to Jackson. Could the kidnapper have been the birth father? If an investigation was opened, could the birth mother change her mind and take her son away?

"Can you give a description of the man from this morning?" Tommy asked.

"Everything happened so fast. All I can remember is that he was wearing a hoodie and a high turtleneck. He was medium height and had these beady dark eyes against olive skin. It didn't look like he'd shaved in a few days. That's about all I can remember," she said.

"It's a start," Tommy said, and his words were reassuring.

He turned to Dallas with that same questioning look.

"He was young and I didn't recognize his voice, so I don't think he's from around here," Dallas added.

"Is it possible that he's the father? If he's not local, then maybe he just found out about the baby and tracked us down," Kate said, fear racing through her at the thought.

"We can't rule it out, but that's just one of many possibilities," Tommy said. "What about your neighbors on Main? I heard some of them weren't too thrilled when you moved in."

"That's the truth," she said.

"Someone might have tried to scare you enough to get you to close shop and leave town. That's a best-case scenario, as far as I'm concerned, because it would mean they never intended to hurt you or the baby. I need a list of names of family, friends, anyone who you've had a disagreement with, and your employees."

The last part caught her off guard. *Employees?*

That had been Dallas's first suspicion, too.

"Sheriff Johnson, you don't seriously think one of my people could be involved, do you?" she asked, not able to fathom the possibility that one of her own could've turned on her.

"Please, call me Tommy," he said. "And I have to search for all possible connections to the guy we're looking for. You'd be surprised what you find out about the people you think you know best."

In his line of work, she could only imagine how true that statement was. How horrible that anyone she trusted might've been involved.

No, it had to be a stranger.

"I have received threats from some of my business neighbors," she said.

"Tell me more about those," Tommy said, leaning forward.

"A few of the other tenants got together to file a complaint with my landlord. They said they didn't think Main was the appropriate place for a soup kitchen," she explained.

"And what was his response?" Tommy asked.

"He didn't do anything. Said as long as my rent was paid on time and I wasn't doing anything illegal, it wasn't anyone else's concern," she said.

"I'll send one of my deputies to canvass the other tenants and see what he can find out. We'll cover all bases with our investigation." Tommy glanced up from his pad. "How long ago did they make the complaint?"

"Right after we first moved in, so about six months ago," she said.

"Anyone make a formal complaint since?"

She shook her head.

"What about direct threats?" Tommy asked.

"Walter Higgins threatened to force me out of town," she said. "But that was a while ago."

"The town needs your services," Dallas said through clenched teeth. "What kind of jerks complain about a person doing something good for others?"

Jackson stirred at the sound of the loud voice and Kate had to find his binky to pacify him. She shuffled through the diaper bag and came up with it. Jackson settled down as soon as the offering was in his mouth.

"Sorry," Dallas said with an apologetic glance.

"It takes all kinds," Tommy agreed. "I'm guessing

they figured it would hurt their business. We'll know more once my deputy speaks to them."

"It's not like people hang around after they eat. There's no loitering allowed downtown," Kate said.

"It's a big escalation to go from complaining to your landlord to a personal attack like this on your son." Based on the sheriff's tone, her neighbors weren't serious suspects. Tommy fired off a text before returning his gaze to Kate. "Now tell me more about your people."

"We have a small office staff," she conceded. "Allen Lentz is my second in command and takes care of everything when I'm not around. Other than that, there are about a dozen cooks and food service workers. Only one is on payroll. The others are volunteers."

Dallas's posture tensed when she mentioned Allen.

Kate registered the subtle change and moved on. She rattled off a few more names and job descriptions.

The sheriff nodded and jotted a few notes on his palm-sized notebook.

"And then there's Randy Ruiz. He keeps the place running on our tight budget. He's our general handyman, muscle and overall miracle worker. Anything heavy needs lifting, he's our guy. He's been especially helpful and dependable in the six months he's been with us." Despite Randy's past, she knew full well that he would never hurt her or Jackson.

Dallas seemed to perk up and she was afraid she'd tried to sell Randy a little too hard. True, she could be a little overprotective of him. He'd had a hard road and she wanted to see him succeed.

"Tabitha Farmer does all our administrative work," Kate added quickly, to keep the conversation moving. "Her official title is volunteer coordinator."

"How close are you with donors?" Tommy asked.

Thinking about the possibility that anyone in her circle could have arranged to have her child kidnapped was enough to turn Kate's stomach. She clasped him closer.

For Jackson's sake, she had to consider what Dallas and the sheriff were saying no matter how much she hated to view her friends and acquaintances with a new lens.

Maybe she was being naive, but she'd been careful to fill her life with genuine people since moving to Bluff from the city. "I maintain a professional distance. However, I do get invited to personal events like weddings and lake house parties."

"And what do you do with your son during these outings?" Dallas interjected, no doubt remembering her conversation with Allen earlier.

"I don't usually go. But I used Allen once," she replied.

"Allen?" Dallas looked up from intensely staring into his cup of coffee.

"We're like a family at the kitchen, and we take care of each other," she said defensively.

Dallas's cocked eyebrow didn't sit well with her. She could feel herself getting more and more defensive.

"Despite what you may be thinking about my employees, they really are a group of decent people," she stated, making eye contact with him—a mistake she was going to regret, given how much her body reacted to the handsome cowboy.

"In my experience, that doesn't always prove the truth," he said, holding her gaze. "When did Allen babysit for you?"

"It's been a while. I used Tabitha one other time recently."

"There a reason for that?" Dallas asked, lifting one dark eyebrow.

"Yes, but it doesn't mean anything," she said quickly. Then she sighed. "Okay, I thought Allen was getting a little too…involved with me and Jackson, so I thought it would be best to use Tabitha instead. He's made it clear that he'd like to date." She involuntarily shivered at the thought of going out with anyone, much less someone from work. "And I'm just not ready for that."

She'd probably emphasized that last bit a little too much, but what did she care if they knew she wasn't in the mood to spend time with a man, any man.

"How old is your son?" Tommy asked, after a few uncomfortable seconds had passed.

"Jackson? He's almost three months old." Kate gently patted her baby on the back, noticing something stir in Dallas's eyes.

"What about friends and family?" Tommy asked, his gaze moving from her to his friend. "Anyone in the area?"

"I didn't know anyone when I moved here, and everything about preparing for the baby was harder than I expected, so, yes, I bonded with my employees."

"You don't have family in this part of Texas?" Tommy asked.

"It's just me and Jackson." She shook her head. "My brother and I are close, but he lives in Richardson, which is a suburb of Dallas. He works nonstop. We started a tech company together after college and made enough to do okay. I sold my interest in the business to have a baby, and now he's running it alone."

"Forgive this question…" Tommy hesitated before continuing, "But how did your brother take the news about you leaving the business the two of you started?"

"Carter? He was fine with my decision. He knew how much I wanted to start a family," she said defensively, a red rash crawling up her neck. And if he hadn't been the most enthusiastic about her choice at first, he'd come around.

"Again, I'm sorry. I had to ask," the sheriff murmured, taking a seat across from her in the sitting area of the office.

"Mind if I ask why you decided to move to Bluff?" Dallas asked.

"There was a need for a soup kitchen, and it's one of the most family-friendly towns in Texas three years running, according to the internet," she said with a shrug. "I thought it would be a good place to bring up a baby."

"Even without family here?" Tommy asked.

"My parents didn't approve of my decision to have a child alone." She didn't really want to go down that road again, explaining the quirks of her family to a stranger. The one where her mother had flipped out and pretended to have a heart attack in order to alter Kate's course.

She glanced at Dallas, ready to defend herself to him, and was surprised by the look of sympathy she got instead.

"I guess I don't understand that particular brand of thinking. It's my personal belief that families should stick together even if they don't agree with each other's decisions," Dallas said, his steely voice sliding right through her.

The sincerity in those words nearly brought her to tears.

Why did it suddenly matter so much what a stranger thought about her or her family?

DALLAS NOTICED KATE'S emotional reaction to what he'd said about family. If she really was at odds with hers then they couldn't rule them out as suspects.

"If you'll excuse us, I'd like to speak to the sheriff in the hallway for a minute," he said to her.

"Do we have to wait around? Can we go home now?" she asked, clearly rattled from their conversation.

"I don't think it's safe," Dallas said, before Tommy could answer. "This attack was ambush-style and planned."

His friend was already nodding in agreement. "The kidnapper had a knife and a getaway vehicle," he added. "This indicates premeditation. I'll need to run this scenario through the database and see if there are similar incidents out there. In the meantime, I'd like to send a deputy to your house to take a look around."

Kate gasped and the baby stirred. She immediately went into action, soothing the infant in her arms. He was such a tiny thing and looked so fragile.

"You think they know where I live?" she asked when the baby had settled into the crook of her arm.

"It's a possibility we can't ignore, and I'd rather be safe than sorry," Tommy said.

"Can I see you in the hallway?" Dallas asked Tommy as his friend rose to his feet. Dallas's protective instincts were kicking into high gear.

"If you're going into the hall to discuss my case, I have a right to know what's being said." Kate's gaze held steady with determination.

Dallas paused at the doorjamb. He couldn't deny that she was right, and yet he wanted to protect her and the baby from hearing what he needed to ask Tommy next.

"Whatever it is, I deserve to hear it," she insisted.

A deep sigh pushed out of his lungs as he turned toward her and stepped back inside, motioning for Tommy to do the same. "The person who did this could be someone who sees Jackson as in the way of being with you," Dallas said, and it seemed to dawn on her that he was talking about Allen.

"Is that why you zeroed in on Allen when I called him earlier?" she asked Dallas pointedly.

"Yes," he answered truthfully.

"We won't stop searching for whoever is behind

this," Tommy interjected. "And we're considering all possibilities."

She sat there for a long moment. "What about those other possibilities, Sheriff?" she finally asked.

"It could be that someone wants revenge against you. It's obvious that your child is very important to you and that snatching him would be one way to hurt you," Tommy said. "Or a teen mom has changed her mind about giving up her child. She might've figured out who you were and told the father."

"The adoption was sealed based on the mother's request. However, I made sure of it to avoid that very circumstance. How on earth would she know where Jackson is?" Kate asked.

"You can find out anything with enough money or computer hacking skills," Dallas answered, even though he knew firsthand either option could take time. And in this case, maybe it had. Jackson was nearly three months old, so that would give someone plenty of time to find the two of them. Grease the right wheels and boom.

"I have to think that if this was a teen mother, then she'd be destitute. Wouldn't she? If she had money or family support, would she really be giving up her baby in the first place?" Kate asked.

Good points.

"How well did you vet this adoption agency before you used them?" Dallas asked.

"They're legitimate, from everything I could tell. I

hired a lawyer to oversee things on my end and make sure everything was legal," Kate stated.

"I'll need the name of your lawyer," Tommy said.

"William Seaver."

"Is he someone you knew or was that the first time you'd dealt with him?" Tommy asked.

"My brother connected us. He'd heard of Seaver through a mutual friend. I'm sure he checked him out first," Kate replied.

"I'll run his name and see if we come up with anything in the database," Tommy offered. "We'll be able to narrow down the possibilities once I get all this information into the system and talk to a few people. Also, I'd like to send someone to take a look at your work computers. I need permission from you in order to do that."

Kate gave her consent even though she seemed reluctant. Her reaction was understandable given the circumstances. Dallas would feel the same way if someone wanted to dig around in the ranch's books.

Tommy called for Abigail.

The older woman appeared a moment later and he asked her to send someone to Kate's house to look for anything suspicious, and after that to run information through the database to see if she got a hit on any similar crimes.

As soon as she left, Dallas turned to Kate. "That's everything I wanted to ask or say about your case. If you'll excuse us, I need to discuss a personal matter with the sheriff."

Dallas motioned for his friend to follow him down the hall and into the kitchenette.

"I'm sorry we lost the guy earlier," Tommy said once they were out of earshot. "If we'd caught him, this nightmare could be over for her."

"Whoever it was seems to know how to disappear pretty darn quick," Dallas commented.

"It's difficult to hide something that weighs more than four thousand pounds," Tommy agreed, obviously referring to the minivan.

"You think this whole thing might've been a setup to scare her out of town?" Dallas asked, unsure of how to approach the subject of his possible fatherhood to his friend.

"I thought about that, as well," he admitted. "It's too early to rule anything out even though it's not likely. I'm anxious to see if we find similar crimes in the database. And, of course, we'll look at her personal circles."

Dallas leaned against the counter and folded his arms across his chest. "I've been looking into adoption agencies myself lately."

"Come again?" Tommy's eyebrows arched and Dallas couldn't blame his friend for the surprised glance he shot him. "I know you're not looking to adopt."

"You remember Susan," Dallas began, uneasy about bringing this up. Susan had grown up in Bluff, so Tommy knew her well.

"So glad you finally saw through her and moved on." His friend rolled his eyes. "She was a head case."

Dallas couldn't argue. His judgment had slipped on that one. As soon as he'd figured her out, he'd broken it off. "She might be more than that. She might be the mother of my child."

The possibility that Dallas could be that careless had never occurred to his friend, a fact made clear by the shock on his face. "There's no way you could've done that!" he declared. "Have you considered the possibility that she's lying?"

"Of course I have," Dallas retorted.

"If this is true, and I'm not convinced it is, where is she? And why didn't you come to me before?" Tommy asked.

"Those are good questions," Dallas admitted. "As far as where she went, I'm looking to find an answer. She disappeared from New Mexico and not even her family here in Bluff has seen her since. We both know that she loved it here. Why wouldn't she come back?"

"She didn't say anything to you before she left?" Tommy folded his arms, his forehead wrinkled in disbelief.

"And I didn't get a chance to ask where she was headed before she disappeared."

"What makes you think she used an adoption agency?" Tommy said, after carefully considering the bomb that had just been dropped. "And why *didn't* you come to me sooner?"

"She told me she was pregnant and said we should get married right away," Dallas said. "I told her to hold on. That I would be there for my child, but that didn't mean we needed to make a mistake."

"That probably went over as well as a cow patty in

the pool." His friend grunted. "She seemed bent on signing her name 'O'Brien' from when we were kids."

Dallas had been an idiot not to see through her quicker.

"But that still doesn't answer my question of why you didn't come to me right away," Tommy said.

"I needed answers. You have to follow the letter of the law," Dallas said honestly. "I wanted someone who could see those lines as blurry."

Tommy took a sip of his coffee. "That the only reason?"

"I knew you'd want to help, and you have a lot of restrictions. I wanted fast answers and I wasn't even sure there'd be anything to discuss," Dallas said. "Plus I didn't want to tell anyone until I was sure."

"Didn't you suspect she was seeing someone else?" his friend asked.

Dallas nodded. "I'm certain she was. I figured she was making a bid for my money when she played the pregnancy card with me."

"She probably was." Tommy grimaced. "Which was a good reason for her to disappear when you refused to marry her. She couldn't get caught in her lies."

"I thought of that, too. There's another thing. I used protection, but it's more than that. We didn't exactly… It's not like…" Hell, this was awkward. Dallas didn't make a habit out of talking about his sex life with anyone, not even his best friend. "There was only the one time with Susan and me. Afterward, she got clingy and tried to move into my place. Started trying to rearrange furniture. I caught her in lie after lie and broke it off clean after I witnessed her in the parking lot with that other guy, looking cozy. I'd suspected she was seeing someone else and she got all cagey when I confronted her and asked her to leave. I couldn't prove my suspicion, though. But when she called a few months later and said she was pregnant with my child, I didn't believe her."

"I can't blame you there," Tommy said. "I wouldn't have bought it, either."

"But I can't turn my back until I know for sure." If what Susan said was true, then he'd already messed up what he considered to be the most important job in life—fatherhood.

Dallas had known Susan could be dishonest, and that was the reason he'd broken it off with her. He couldn't love someone he couldn't trust. But he never imagined she'd lie about something this important.

"If there was another guy involved, and I believe you when you say there was, then he could be the father of her child." Tommy sipped his coffee, contemplating what he had just learned.

"You know I can't walk away until I know one way or the other," Dallas said. "This isn't something I can leave to chance."

"And there was that one time," his friend finally said, his forehead pinched with concentration. "So, there is a possibility."

"If I'm honest…yes."

"But it's next to impossible. I know you. There's

no way you would risk a pregnancy unless you were one hundred percent sure about a relationship staying together," he stated.

Dallas nodded.

And then it seemed to dawn on Tommy. "But she could've sabotaged your efforts."

"Right."

"Well, damn." His friend's expression changed to one of pity. "I'm sorry to hear this might've happened. Any idea how old the baby would be now?"

"According to my calculations…about three months old." And that was most likely the reason Kate's case hit him so hard. If he had a son, the boy would be around the same age as Jackson.

"Any idea where Susan and the baby may be? It'd be easy enough to get a paternity test once you find them."

Tommy said the exact thing Dallas was thinking.

"I don't know. Neither does the man I hired to find them. She literally disappeared." Ever since hearing about a possible pregnancy with Susan, Dallas had found his world tipped on its axis and he didn't exactly feel like himself.

"There might not even be a baby," Tommy said.

Dallas's phone buzzed. He fished it out of his pocket and then checked the screen. "Susan had a boy," he said, focusing on the message from his private investigator's assistant, Stacy Miller. "And Morton was able to link her to an adoption agency."

Tommy rubbed his chin, deep in thought.

Yeah, Dallas felt the same way right about now. Especially when the next text came through, and he learned the adoption agency was named Safe Haven.

Chapter Four

"I'd say that's a strange coincidence, but I know Safe
Haven is the biggest agency in the area, so I guess I'm
not too surprised to hear their name again," Tommy
said. "And just because Susan had a baby doesn't mean
it's yours."

"That kid in there is around the age Susan's baby
would be," Dallas supplied.

"Doesn't mean he's Susan's," Tommy said. "Odds
are against it."

"I know." Dallas nodded, still trying to digest the
news. His plans to help Kate Williams get settled with
the sheriff and then head back to the ranch to start a
busy day exploded. They had a record number of bred
heifers and there'd be a calf-boom early next year that
everyone was preparing for. But nothing was more
important than this investigation.

"In fact, I'm inclined to think that's the closest thing
we have to proof that the baby isn't yours."

Dallas made a move to speak, but his friend raised
his hand to stop him. "Hear me out. If Susan was telling the truth and the baby was yours, she would stick

around for a DNA test. If she couldn't have your last name, then at least her son would, and he'd have everything that comes with being an O'Brien, which is what we all know she's always wanted anyway."

Dallas thought about those words for a long moment. "I see your point."

"And I'm right."

"Either way, if she used Safe Haven, then everything should be legit, right?" Dallas asked, hoping he'd be able to gain traction and get answers now that a child had been confirmed and he had the name of an adoption agency. His investigator was making good progress.

"They've been investigated before and came up clean." Tommy took another sip of his coffee. "That doesn't mean they are. They could be running an off-the-books program for nontraditional families. Kate's case gives me reason to dig into their records. I'll make a request for access to their files and see how willing they are to cooperate."

"Will you keep me posted on your progress?" Dallas asked, knowing he was asking a lot of his friend.

Tommy nodded. "I'll give you as much information as I legally can."

"As far as Susan goes, you're the only one who knows, and I'd appreciate keeping it between us for now."

"You haven't told anyone in the family?" Tommy asked in surprise.

"Everyone's had enough to deal with since Mom

and Pop..." Dallas didn't finish his sentence. He didn't have to. Tommy knew.

"If you have a child, and I'd bet my life you don't, we'll find him," Tommy said, and his words were meant to be reassuring.

He was the only person apart from Dallas's brothers who would know just how much the prospect would gnaw at him. And if his brothers knew, they'd all want to be involved, but Dallas didn't want to sound the alarm just yet. There might not be anything to discuss, and he didn't like getting everyone riled up without cause.

Another text came through on his phone.

"Looks like my guy left to investigate Safe Haven last night and hasn't checked in for work this morning," Dallas murmured. "His assistant said he's always the first one in the office. She's been texting and calling him and he isn't responding."

"We need to talk to her," Tommy said. "You know I'm going to offer my help investigating Susan's disappearance. She's originally from here and that makes her my business."

"And I'll take it," Dallas declared. He wouldn't rely solely on Tommy, because his friend was bound by laws. Dallas saw them more as guidelines when it came to finding out the truth. "We can work both cases and share information. As far as Kate's goes, I'm not sure I like Allen Lentz."

The sheriff leaned against the counter with a questioning look on his face.

"He sounded possessive of her when she called him

this morning, and I got the impression he sees the kid as an obstacle to dating her," Dallas explained. The news that Susan had had a boy was still spinning around in the back of his mind.

"I'll have one of my deputies bring him in for questioning this morning," Tommy said. "See if I can get a feel for the guy."

"I'd be interested to hear your take on him," Dallas stated. "I told her not to clue him in to what had happened this morning when she phoned him to open the kitchen for her. And I asked her to put him on speaker so I could hear his voice."

"What was your impression of how he sounded?"

"I didn't like the guy one bit." Dallas would keep the part about feeling a twinge of jealousy to himself.

"Wanting the kid out of the way would give him motive," Tommy said. "I'll run a background check on him when I bring him in. See if there's anything there."

Tommy's phone buzzed. "This is my deputy," he said, after glancing at the screen.

Dallas motioned for them to return to Kate as his friend answered the call.

She was cradling the baby and Dallas got another glimpse of the little boy's black curly hair—hair that looked a lot like his own—as they walked into the office. Dallas wasn't quite ready to accept that possibility completely as he moved closer to get a better look at Jackson. There was no way that Kate's son could be Susan's baby.

Right?

Tommy was right. All of this would be way too much

of a coincidence. The adoption agency was large and there had to be dozens of dark-haired baby boys who had been adopted around the same time. Not that logic mattered at a time like this.

Plus, Dallas hadn't considered the fact that if Susan had had his baby, then wouldn't she sue him for support? Or blackmail him to keep the news out of the press?

Until he could be certain, would Dallas look at every boy around Jackson's age with the same question: Could the child be his?

Not knowing would be mental torture at its worst. Every dark-haired boy he came across would get Dallas's mind spinning with possibilities. What-ifs. Was he getting a glimpse of the torment he'd endure for the rest of his life if he couldn't find Susan?

Morton had confirmed there'd been a child, which didn't necessarily mean Dallas was a father. And Morton had been able to link Susan to Safe Haven Adoption Agency. Dallas had every reason to believe that his PI would figure out the rest and Dallas would get his answers very soon. Being in limbo, not knowing, would eat what was left of his stomach lining.

Kate was watching him with a keen eye as Tommy entered the room.

"Can I go home now?" she asked, cradling Jackson tighter.

"This might sound like an odd question, but do you close and lock your doors when you leave your house?" Tommy asked.

"Yes. Of course. I'm a single woman who lives

alone with a baby, and I wouldn't dream of leaving myself vulnerable like that," she said, and her cheeks flushed.

Embarrassment?

Dallas noted the emotion as his friend moved on. "Well, then, your place has been broken into," Tommy said.

"What happened?" Kate's face paled.

Dallas's first thought was Allen. But wouldn't he already have access to her house?

Not if she never let him inside. Maybe the date bit was a ruse to get into her home.

"The back door was ajar and the lock had been tampered with. My deputy on the scene said that nothing obvious is missing inside. All the pictures are on the walls and the place is neat." Tommy listened and then said a few "uh-huh"s into the phone.

"Do you have a home computer?" he asked Kate.

"A laptop on my desk," she answered.

Tommy repeated the information to his deputy and then frowned.

So, someone took her laptop?

"Are you sure it was on your desk the last time you saw it?" Tommy asked.

"Certain. Why? Is it gone?"

He nodded. "The cable is still there."

That same look of fear and disbelief filled her blue eyes.

"Can you think of anything on your hard drive someone would want?" Tommy asked. He also asked about work files, but Dallas figured whoever broke into her house wasn't going after those. This had to be personal, especially after the failed kidnapping attempt.

If someone was trying to scare her, then he was doing a great job of it, based on her expression.

"No. Nothing. I keep all my work stuff at the office. I vowed not to work at home ever again once I left the corporate scene. I have a manila file folder in the drawer, right-hand side, about Jackson's adoption," she added, holding tighter to her baby. "Is it missing?"

Once again Tommy relayed the information and then waited. "There's nothing labeled Safe Haven or Adoption," he said at last.

"Then that's it," she murmured, almost too quietly to hear.

Tommy thanked his deputy and ended the call. "How did you get connected with Safe Haven?"

"Through my lawyer. He was the one who arranged everything," she said, and based on her expression, Dallas figured her brain was most likely clicking through possibilities.

He made a mental note that they needed to speak to her brother, and the rest of her family, as well. Dallas didn't like to think that her family wouldn't be 100 percent supportive of her choices, but he wasn't stupid. He couldn't fathom it, but if her mother was really against the adoption, then she could be trying to interfere by shaking Kate up. Maybe even hoping that she'd realize she'd made a mistake.

If that were true, then Kate's mother hadn't seen the woman holding Jackson.

A family intervention, albeit misguided, would be

so much better than the other options Kate faced. Such as an employee's fixation or the fact that this could've been a shady adoption gone bad for Safe Haven.

KATE HELD ON to Jackson as if he'd drop off a canyon wall if she let go. She'd walked away from the only life she'd ever known to have a chance at a family. Her husband, Robert Bass, had filed for divorce within weeks of learning that she had a 4 percent chance of ever getting pregnant. Four percent.

Half the reason she'd worked so hard at the start-up was so she could sell her interests when she became pregnant and be home with the baby. And then suddenly that wasn't going to be an option, ever.

At thirty-three, she'd had everything she thought she wanted, a nice house, a Suburban and a husband. She'd believed she was on the track to happiness, and it was easy to ignore shortcomings in her marriage to Robert considering how much time she spent at the office. He worked all the time, too.

Within weeks of learning the devastating news, her entire life had turned upside down, and all she could do was kick herself for not seeing it coming earlier. All those times Robert had decided to stay late at the office even when she'd made special arrangements to leave early… And she'd been too busy to really notice how frequent his ski trips had become—ski trips she later realized hadn't been with his best friend, but with his coworker Olivia Gail.

In fact, he'd been on the road more than he was

home and Kate felt like an idiot for thinking he was working hard to secure a future for their family, too.

Whatever love had been between them had died long before she'd been willing to acknowledge it. Or had she kept herself too busy to notice? Too busy to face the reality of the loneliness that had become her life?

She'd been trapped with a husband who cared for her but didn't love her. And the worst part was that she'd kept convincing herself that they'd be able to get back what they'd had in the early days of their relationship as soon as she had more time or had a baby. How crazy was it to think a child would somehow make things better, make them a family?

To make matters worse, Kate Williams didn't give up. Hard work and staying the course had made her business a success. It had gotten her through a difficult childhood with a mother who was bent on controlling her. Was her mother's lack of real love the reason Kate had fallen for Robert in the first place? Was she seeking approval from someone who would never give it?

Robert had been all about keeping his tee time and staying on track with his future career plans. He even seemed content to have a family with Kate though he no longer loved her.

And then when the disappointing news had come that having a baby would be next to impossible, he'd started traveling even more. He'd lost interest in her sexually.

Kate had reasoned that he needed time to process the news, as she did. It was a bomb she'd never expected to be dropped on her, especially not when her biological clock wouldn't expire for years.

Robert's decision to give up on the marriage shouldn't have come as a complete shock. Except that she'd ignored or made excuses for every single one of the signs that it was coming.

Given the amount of time he had spent calculating return on investment with his stock portfolio, she should've realized he'd cut his losses with her when she was no longer a good deal. Apparently, she hadn't been worth the risk. It had taken Robert about six weeks to divest himself of her.

Kate had signed the divorce papers and then made a life-changing decision.

She was going to have a family anyway.

When she'd told Carter, her brother, he'd scoffed at the idea, initially telling her to take a long vacation instead. Then he'd reminded her how much she'd be hurting their mother, as if Charlotte Williams hadn't already made her position clear throughout the whole divorce. Chip and Charlotte had been the perfect parents, to hear her mother talk about their life.

Kate had been clear on what she wanted, and being a mother had more to do with love than DNA, so she'd decided to adopt.

Carter came to his senses, apologized and then located the best adoption attorney he could find.

Not long after, Kate had sold her interests in the company and moved to Bluff.

Life might have thrown her a twist, but that didn't mean she had to roll over and take it.

The move had given her a new lease on life. Becoming Jackson's mother was the greatest joy she'd experienced. And, dammit, no one would take that or him away from her.

A voice she immediately recognized as Allen's boomed from the other room.

Kate popped to her feet. "Why's he here?" she asked, glancing from Tommy to Dallas.

"I'll be interviewing everyone on your staff," the sheriff said, drawing her gaze back to him. "Would your family members be willing to come down and speak to us, as well?"

"My family?" she echoed, as Allen walked into the office.

"What's going on?" he asked, concern widening his eyes as he zeroed in on Kate and the baby.

Dallas stepped in front of her, blocking his path.

"Did something happen?" Allen shouted over him. "Are you okay?"

"I'm fine now," she said, hating that her employees would be worried.

"Will someone please tell me what's going on?" Allen begged, and there was desperation in his voice as he was being hauled away.

DALLAS POSITIONED HIMSELF near the two-way mirror on the other side of the interview room. His cup of coffee had long ago gone cold, but holding on to it gave him something to do with his hands.

"Miss Williams authorized my department to take a look at your computer," Tommy said to Allen.

"So what?" The confusion on the guy's face was either an award-worthy acting job or he really didn't have a clue.

"Would you agree to give one of my deputies access to your house?" Tommy asked. He knew full well that an innocent guy would have nothing to hide.

"Not until you tell me what this is about," Allen retorted.

Fair enough.

"We're looking for information that will aid an ongoing investigation," Tommy hedged.

"One that involves my boss." It wasn't a question.

The lawman nodded.

"Look, I would do anything to help Kate. She's like family to me," Allen said. "But I have no idea what's going on."

So asking out a family member was okay in Allen's book? Dallas covered up his cough.

"And I'm not sure how invading my privacy will accomplish your mission, so I'm afraid you'll have to tell me a little bit more about what you think you'll find," Allen added.

Dallas had been sure this guy was guilty as sin, but something was gnawing at him and he couldn't figure out what. He might be covering for a crush he had on his boss and didn't want to be embarrassed any further.

Based on his actions so far, Allen was coming across as a concerned friend. But then, he might just be that good at acting.

Dallas returned to Tommy's office, where Kate waited.

"How long has Allen worked for you?" he asked.

"He was my first hire," she said, looking as if she was about to be sick. "So, about six months now."

"Do want water or something else to drink?" Dallas asked.

She shook her head and mumbled that she was fine. Tommy walked in.

"How would you characterize your relationship with Allen Lentz?" he asked Kate.

"Professional," she retorted.

"I had to ask." Tommy brought his hand up defensively.

"But he wasn't kidding about our office being like a family. Do you really think he broke into my house and stole my laptop and adoption files?" she asked Tommy, looking as if she was trying to let that possibility sink in.

"Not completely, no," he answered. "It doesn't mean he's not involved, though. The kidnapping attempt could've been a distraction while the burglar got what he really wanted."

Kate pinched the bridge of her nose as though staving off a headache.

Tommy's cell buzzed. He glanced at the screen. "If you'll excuse me."

Kate nodded as Tommy hurried out of the room.

Dallas didn't say that none of this added up quite in the way he wanted it to. All her employees would know that she was already at the soup kitchen. If someone wanted her laptop and adoption files, all he had to do was break in while she was gone. But it was clear that her adoption was at the center of the kidnapping attempt. Could someone be trying to erase the paperwork trail? "Do you ever go back to your place after leaving for work?"

"Not unless I've forgotten something for Jackson," she said.

"Do you normally take him to work with you?" Dallas asked.

"Yes. And then Mrs. Zilker picks him up, although sometimes she sticks around the office for a while," Kate stated. "Oh, no. I forgot to let her know I don't need her today."

"Then someone could've been trying to make sure you didn't go back home," Dallas said.

"I hope that's all it is and not the fact that someone wants to take Jackson away from me." Kate clutched him closer, as if daring anyone to try.

"If Allen will agree to let a deputy search his house, then that'll go a long way toward clearing him," Dallas said.

"I hope he does so we can cross him off the suspect list," she said, and she sounded as if she really didn't want her friend to be involved, more than that she was convinced he wasn't.

Tommy entered the room with a stark expression.

Dallas didn't like the look on his friend's face.

"What is it?" he asked.

"A vehicle registered to Wayne Morton was found abandoned off of Farm Road 23," Tommy said, a look of apology in his eyes. "They found blood spatter but no sign of a body."

"I'm guessing there's no other indication of Morton anywhere?" Dallas asked. But he already knew the answer to that question and an ominous feeling settled over him. Between the blood spatter and the fact that Morton hadn't checked in with his assistant this morning, Dallas feared the worst. "We need to talk to Stacy to find out what she knows about his itinerary."

"No. I need to talk to his assistant," Tommy said. "I can send a deputy to Morton's office."

"Might be best if I speak to her personally. She might open up to me more than a stranger," Dallas suggested. He felt guilt settle heavy on his shoulders, knowing that if anything had happened to Morton it could be his fault. History would be repeating itself. He muttered a curse too low for anyone else to hear.

"Does this have anything to do with my case?" Kate asked. "Because if it does, I'd like to go with you."

"No," Dallas said. "You should stay here in the sheriff's office just to be safe."

He hadn't anticipated the uncomfortable feeling he got in his gut at the thought of leaving her. She'd be in good hands with Tommy and yet he felt the need to stick around and watch over her. He told himself that it was all protective instinct and had nothing to do with the sizzle of attraction he felt when she was near.

"Hold on a sec. Did Lentz give you permission to search his place?" Dallas asked Tommy, figuring it would be good to rule out one suspect.

His friend said, "No."

"Are you done questioning him?" Dallas pressed.

Tommy frowned. "He lawyered up."

Chapter Five

"Deputy Lopez just briefed me on the computer search at the soup kitchen," Tommy said to Dallas. "Turns out that Allen Lentz has an unusual amount of pictures of Ms. Williams on cloud storage that we accessed via his computer."

Dallas didn't like the sound of that.

"He takes all the office party photos." Kate jumped to Lentz's defense.

Abigail knocked on the door to Tommy's office and all eyes focused on her. "There have been six other kidnappings in the past three weeks in Texas, all boys, all adopted and all at gunpoint."

"He used a knife with me," Kate stated, shivering at the thought that it could've been worse.

"The first infant was found three days later in a car seat on the steps of his day care center," she said. "The second and third were found several days after their disappearances, under similar circumstances."

"Three are still missing?" Tommy asked.

His secretary nodded. "The three most recent ones."

"Was there a ransom demand in any of the cases?" Tommy asked.

"Not once," she stated.

"Have Deputy Solomon check into the incidences to see if we can find a link to Safe Haven," Tommy said.

Kate perked up. "That means Allen is innocent, right?"

The sheriff looked from Dallas to her apologetically. "Not necessarily. He could be mimicking other kidnappings to distract attention away from him. The MO was different with you and I can't rule anyone out until I know why."

"To be clear, someone is taking babies who are the same sex and around the same age with no ransom demand and then making sure they're found a couple of days later?" Dallas asked Tommy.

"I'm inclined to draw the same conclusion," Tommy said. "The kidnappers are looking for a specific child."

Abigail moved to Kate, motioning toward Jackson. "Let me take him in the other room where he can sleep peacefully."

Kate stilled.

"I'll take good care of him. Don't you worry," Abigail assured her. "He's in good hands with me."

"Thank you." She handed over her sleeping baby. "So the pictures you found on Allen's computer aren't office pictures, are they?" she said, sinking back into the chair.

"No, ma'am." Tommy waved her and Dallas over

to his desk and then pulled up a file on his computer, positioning the monitor for all three of them to see.

One by one, pictures of Kate filled the screen.

"These were taken in my house," she said, shock evident in her voice.

"Actually, from outside your house, like through a window," Dallas observed.

"He's been watching me?" Her hand covered her mouth as she gasped. "Pictures of me sleeping?"

The questions were rhetorical, and the hurt and disbelief audible in them was like a punch to Dallas's gut.

He reached out to comfort her, not expecting her to spin around into his arms and bury her face in his chest.

This close, he felt her body trembling. A curse tore from his lips as he pulled her nearer, ignoring how soft her skin was or how well she fitted in his arms. His attraction to her was going to be a problem if he didn't keep it in check.

"Sheriff, can I see you in the hallway for a moment?" Deputy Lopez peeked inside the door.

Tommy agreed and then shot a warning look toward Dallas. He was telling him not to get too close to the victim, and Dallas couldn't ignore the fact that it was sound advice.

He had moved past logic and gone straight to primal instinct the second her body pressed to his.

But he wasn't stupid enough to confuse this for anything more than what it was for her—comfort from a stranger.

The sudden urge to lift her chin and capture her

mouth with his wasn't logical, either. But Dallas couldn't regret it the instant her pink lips pressed against his.

Her arms came up to his chest, her palms flat against his pecs.

As if they both suddenly realized where they were and that someone could walk through that door at any second, they pulled back, hearts pounding in rhythm.

Chemistry sizzled between them, charging the air.

Tommy walked in and his tense expression signaled more bad news.

"Two things," he stated. "First, Morton's body has been found floating in the lake on the Hatches' property. He'd been fatally shot, but the perp tied a bag of heavy rocks around his midsection."

"Amateurs?" Dallas asked.

"It would appear so," Tommy agreed. "And it looks like they did this on the spur of the moment, using whatever they could find."

"What else?" Dallas was trying to digest this news. He was the one who'd gotten Morton involved in this case and now the PI was dead. Guilt sat heavy on his chest as he tried to take a breath.

"The other news—" he glanced from Dallas to Kate "—is that more pictures were found at Lentz's place. A lot of them."

"And that would confirm his fixation on Kate," Dallas said, which was the logical assumption. But he had a gnawing feeling that the guy was innocent. Dallas wanted him to be guilty. That would tie this whole troubling case up with a bow. Lentz would be arrested. Kate and Jackson would be safe. Problem solved.

And yet Dallas worried this was more complicated.

Babies were going missing. Investigating Safe Haven had most likely cost Morton his life. Anger pierced Dallas, leaving a huge hole in his chest.

Kate took a step back, grabbing the desk to steady herself. "What kind of pictures?"

"Just like the ones you saw earlier," Tommy said. "And there were ones with markings across Jackson's face."

Kate gasped again, looking stunned. "I can't believe Allen would do something like that. I know I saw the photos with my own eyes, but it doesn't make any sense."

As much as Dallas didn't like the guy, part of him agreed with Kate. This was too easy. "Does Allen have any enemies? Did he get into a fight with anyone lately?"

Someone could be setting up Lentz. But who? And why?

Her lips pressed together and Dallas forced himself not to stare. Thinking about that kiss was inappropriate as hell and yet there it was anyway.

"The baby keeps me busy. I don't really socialize with anyone outside of work, so I couldn't say for sure about his personal life." She shot an apologetic look toward Tommy. "He didn't talk about having any arguments and no one's been around the soup kitchen."

"Kate!" The anguish in Allen's voice shattered the silence in the hallway. "Let me talk to Kate. Those aren't my pictures. I don't know where they came from. I'm being set up."

Dallas heard one of the deputies shuffling Lentz down the hall, most likely to a jail cell.

"I would never do something like this. I love Jackson," the man shouted, and it visibly shook Kate.

She glanced around the room. "I honestly don't know what to say. I have no idea who would do this to him, and even though those pictures completely creep me out, I still can't believe he would do something like this."

Dallas rubbed his chin. "It would have to be someone with access to his computer at work and at his home."

Kate gripped the desk. "There's one person I can think of who would have access to both, but there's no way he would do anything like this."

Dallas nodded, urging her to keep talking.

"My handyman, Randy Ruiz," she finally said and then bit her bottom lip.

"I'll check him out." Tommy typed the name into the system. "We ran Lentz earlier and his background check came up clean, by the way."

"And Ruiz?" Dallas asked.

"He has a record," Tommy noted, staring at his computer screen.

"I know. I knew that when I hired him. But that was a long time ago, and good people deserve a second chance," Kate said. "He's never been so much as late to work, let alone missed a day. He has a wonderful family."

And a rap sheet, Dallas thought.

Tommy locked gazes with him. "Ruiz has a history of burglary."

"So he would know how to get in and out of a house without anyone seeing him," Dallas confirmed.

"He wouldn't have had to. Allen gave him a copy of his keys so he could fix a leaky pipe in his downstairs bathroom," Kate declared.

Dallas could only imagine how difficult it must be to have to think about the possibility that people she trusted would do something to hurt her. The employees at the ranch were more family than most of Dallas's cousins.

"We need to bring in Ruiz for questioning," Tommy said.

"I'M SO SORRY this is happening, Randy," Kate said to her employee as he was led into the sheriff's office.

"Someone tried to hurt you and little Jackson?" Randy asked, concern lines bracketing his mouth.

"Yes. This morning," she said.

"That's why you weren't at work today?"

She nodded.

"Mrs. Zilker was worried. Allen told her everything was fine and to take the day off," Randy said.

Dallas couldn't help but notice the prison tattoos on the handyman's arms when he took off his jacket. The guy was a five-foot-nine wall of solid muscle. He had clean-cut dark hair and a trim mustache. His genuine worry made him seem far less threatening. And even though his job could have him snaking out a toilet at a moment's notice, his jeans looked new and had been pressed. He definitely fit the bill of someone who cared about doing a good job.

Kate nodded. "I told the sheriff how much you love your job and what an exemplary employee you are," she said to Randy. "I'm so sorry you have to come here and answer questions."

"I'm not," he said emphatically. "If this helps them find the guy who tried to kidnap Jackson, then I want to do everything I can to help."

Kate thanked him.

Based on his serious expression, he meant every word. And that pretty much ruled him out as a suspect, because with his record, Dallas would've thought he'd be offended. His genuine lack of self-concern said he would jump through any hoop if it meant figuring out who was trying to hurt Kate.

But the interview wasn't a total loss. They'd ruled someone out and it was possible that Randy had seen or heard something that could help them figure out if anyone else in the office was involved.

Tommy shot a sideways glance toward Dallas and he immediately knew that his friend thought the same thing.

"I heard about what happened to Allen," Randy said, shaking his head, his slight Hispanic accent barely noticeable.

Interesting word choices, Dallas noted.

"I made mistakes in the past, but I'm a family man now," he said to the sheriff. "Don't waste your time looking at me."

"All I need is for you to answer a few questions so

we can figure out who did this," Tommy replied, a hint of admiration in his eyes.

"Allen's a good guy," Randy said. "He would never do anything to hurt Miss Kate or her baby."

Dallas believed that to be true, too. It was almost too easy to pin this on Lentz. And that made Dallas believe that the guy might have been set up.

"How long did it take Deputy Lopez to find the pictures on Lentz's computer?" Dallas asked Tommy.

"Not long. Why?" his friend asked.

"How good is Allen with computers?" Dallas asked Randy, and Tommy's nod of approval said he'd figured out where Dallas was going with this.

"That man knows his way around them for sure. He helps me all the time with the one I have at home for my kids," the handyman said.

Dallas turned to Kate. He needed a reason to rule out Lentz. "How would you classify Allen's computer skills?"

"Very competent," she said, and then it must've dawned on her. "And you're thinking why wouldn't he have password protected those files, aren't you?"

"That's exactly what I'm thinking," he agreed. "I'm sure the deputies could've gotten to those files, given enough time, even if they'd been buried. But it was easy."

"Too easy," Tommy said, "because they weren't hidden at all."

"And then at Allen's house they happen to find even more damning evidence," Dallas said.

Kate was already rocking her head. "The black bars across Jackson's face."

"Let's take a closer look at some of those pics and see if we can get a clue." Tommy moved to his computer and his fingers went to work on the keyboard.

"If not Allen, then who took the pictures?" she wondered.

"Great question," Dallas said.

Tommy clicked through the pictures once again, slowly this time.

"What are you looking for?" Dallas asked.

"Clues to when these pictures were taken. I'm trying to piece together a timeline. It'll take a while to have all the evidence analyzed, but maybe we can figure out a window and then narrow down the possibilities. Kate, can you identify when you wore those pajamas?"

"Hard to tell. I wear something like those most nights." A red blush crawled up her neck to her cheeks.

Randy's gaze immediately dropped to the floor, as if to spare her further embarrassment.

"I can clear the room if you'd be more comfortable doing this alone," Tommy said to her.

"No. It's fine," she said. The red blush on her cheeks belied her words. "I always wear an oversize T-shirt. I rotate between a couple, so that could be any night."

She studied the new picture on the screen. "This one was recent." She pointed to a mug on the side table next to her bed. "I just started drinking tea within the last two weeks."

"Good," Tommy said. "Could most of these pictures have been taken within that time frame?"

"Let's see," she said, studying each one as more flashed across the screen. "Yes. All of them could."

"So, someone gets happy with a camera in the past two weeks and then tries to snatch Jackson, all while pointing the finger at Allen to distract attention from the real person behind this." Dallas summed it up. On a larger scale, baby boys around Jackson's age were being kidnapped and released.

"And then we have the issue of Kate's kidnapping attempt being slightly different than the others," Tommy said, and that was exactly Dallas's next thought. Jackson's kidnapper had used a knife. And someone had broken into her house and stolen her adoption files.

"Were there break-ins at the other houses?" Dallas asked.

Tommy said there weren't.

"I should go." He needed to get over and talk to Stacy, to see what else she knew about Morton.

"I know what you're thinking. I'm coming with you," Tommy said.

"I might get more out of Stacy if I'm on my own," Dallas pointed out. "And I need to follow up with Safe Haven."

"This is a murder investigation, Dallas. I'm going with you or you're not going at all." The lawman's tone left no room for argument.

"I'm coming, too," Kate said. Her eyes fixed on Dallas and all he could see was that same determination he'd noted earlier when someone had been trying to snatch her baby from her arms.

"Absolutely not." He didn't have to think about the answer to that one.

"If this involves Jackson, then I'm coming, and you can't stop me," she said emphatically.

"I don't know if it does or not yet." If someone at the adoption agency was involved in Morton's murder and that same person was after Jackson, the last thing Dallas intended to do was put Kate in harm's way.

"That's the place I adopted him and my files are missing from home," she said. "I have to believe that's not a coincidence."

Maybe not.

"It might be best for you to stay put," Dallas countered. The thought that this could be one of her neighbors died on the vine.

"I don't have to ask your permission. I can go with or without you." She stood her ground. "I have a relationship with them and I have every right to request my file and talk to the people there who were involved in my case."

Dallas blew out a frustrated breath, suspecting that if she went in alone she could be walking into danger. A perp could be watching the place, seeing who came and went to get information.

"Both of you need to calm down," Tommy said. "I don't want either one of you going without me, especially if they're responsible for a murder. You'd be putting yourself in unnecessary danger."

Tommy was right about one thing. Kate had no

business investigating Safe Haven, given what had happened to Morton after he'd started going down that route.

"A man is dead because of me," Dallas said to his friend.

"He was a professional and he knew the risks his job carried," the lawman said soberly.

"I hired him and he was there because of me. I'm responsible for him," Dallas countered, realizing he was arguing with the one man who'd understand taking risks on his job.

"Does this mean Allen is in the clear?" Randy asked.

"It does for now," the sheriff said.

"Good. Then I can give him a ride home."

"Not yet," Tommy said. "I have a few more questions for him, so I want him to stick around."

Dallas stood and thanked the handyman, offering a handshake.

"I know this is asking a lot," Kate interjected, "but could you go back to the office? I have no idea when I'll be able to return, and I want to make sure people are being fed."

"Of course," Randy said. "We'll keep things running until you can come back."

"Thank you!" Kate rose to her feet and gave him a hug. "I'm so sorry that this is happening and I hope you know how much I trust you and the rest of the staff."

"Don't worry about us or the soup kitchen." Randy looked her in the eye. "We're all adults. We can handle this. Just take care of yourself and little Jackson and leave the rest up to us."

Dallas could feel the sense of family in the room. He would know, because he had five brothers who would be saying the same things had they known what was going on.

Which reminded him that he needed to fill them in on his situation with Susan. Just not yet.

With Morton's death, Dallas also realized that Susan could have gotten involved with the wrong people and ended up in over her head. The two of them as a couple didn't work, but he had some residual feelings for her. She was someone he'd dated and at one time had wanted to get to know better. They'd grown up in the same town and had known each other for years. Dallas didn't wish this on anyone and especially not Susan. Baby drama aside, he hoped that she hadn't done something to put herself at risk.

For her sake as much as his, Dallas needed to know what had happened to her and the baby she'd given birth to.

As he started toward the door, he realized that he had no means of transportation. He also realized he had a shadow. Kate was buttoning up her coat as she followed him.

He stopped and she had to put on the brakes in order to avoid walking straight into him. Her flat palms on his back brought a jolt of electricity.

Dallas turned around quickly and Kate took a step back. "My pickup is at the supply store parking lot. Can you take me to it?"

"For the record, I don't like either one of you anywhere near the attempted kidnapping site or Safe Haven," Tommy interjected.

Dallas shot his friend a telling look. "I'm going to talk to Stacy first."

"While you do that, I'll investigate the crime scene," the sheriff conceded. "Keep me posted on what you find out from her and let her know that I'll be stopping by her office for a statement later today."

KATE HATED THE thought of being separated from Jackson, to the point her heart hurt. If leaving to find answers wasn't a trade-off for his ultimate safety, then she wouldn't be able to go, not even knowing he'd be with someone as competent as Abigail. His security had to be the priority.

For a second, Kate considered calling her babysitter, but after this morning's kidnapping attempt there was no way she would risk putting Mrs. Zilker in danger.

Abigail stopped at the doorway, Jackson resting peacefully in her arms. "Walter Higgins is refusing to answer questions without an attorney present."

"He's always been a stubborn one." Tommy shook his head and shrugged. "We'll give it to him his way. Send Deputy Lopez to pick him up and bring him in. I doubt he'll be useful given the turn of events, but I'd like him to know that we're aware of his antics with Ms. Williams."

"Yes, sir."

"Any news about the other incidences?" the sheriff asked.

Her gaze bounced from Kate to him, making the hair on Kate's arms stand on end. "So far, we've been able to make contact with one of the families."

"And?" Tommy asked.

"They adopted their son from Safe Haven almost three months ago," Abigail stated, with an apologetic glance toward Kate.

Kate struggled to breathe as anxiety caused her chest to squeeze.

"Any other obvious connections to our current case?" he continued.

"Other than the fact they've all occurred between Houston and San Antonio?" Abigail asked.

Tommy nodded.

"That's all I have so far," she replied. "We'll know more as we hear back from the other families."

Kate stepped forward and kissed Jackson, praying this would not be the last time she saw him. Then she walked out the door and toward her car.

"We need to switch to my pickup at some point today," Dallas said, once they were in the parking lot.

"Hold on a second. I have a few questions before we leave." She stopped cold. She'd been so distracted by her own problems, she hadn't stopped to really think about everything she'd heard at the sheriff's office.

Dallas turned around and faced her.

"What is your connection to Safe Haven?" she asked.

"I've been helping a close friend figure out if he's

a father or not," he said, and something told her there was more to that story than he was sharing. "He wants to keep his identity out of the papers, so he asked me to help. I hired Morton to investigate and you know the rest from there."

Kate tossed him her keys. No way could she concentrate on driving in her current state.

"My adoption was legal," she said, once she was buckled in. "I followed all the right channels."

Kate pressed her fingers to her temples to stave off the headache threatening.

Dallas glanced at her and then quickly focused on the road again. "When was the last time you ate?"

"Last night, I think," she said. "Guess I shouldn't have had that cup of coffee on an empty stomach. I feel nauseous."

Dallas cut right.

"Where are you going?" she asked.

"Somewhere I can get you something to eat," he said in a don't-argue-with-me tone.

So she didn't. There wouldn't be a point, and Kate didn't have the energy anyway. She'd drained herself putting up enough of a fight to go with him.

"What about your truck?"

"We'll swing by and pick it up after I get food in you."

She expected Dallas to pull into the first fast-food drive-through they saw, but there were none on the route he chose. After a good twenty minutes, she started to ask where he was taking her and then saw the sign for his family's ranch, Cattlemen Crime Club.

"Why are we here?" she asked. Wasn't this too far out of the way?

"Because I need to know that you'll be safe while I feed you," Dallas said, pulling up to the first gate and entering a code. A security officer waved as Dallas passed through the second checkpoint.

"I still think these guys are after Jackson, not me," she countered. "But I won't argue, since we're already here."

Kate didn't want to admit to being curious about Dallas. In fact, she wanted to know more about him, and that was a surprise given that she didn't think it would be possible for her to be interested in another man so soon after Robert.

Interest wasn't necessarily the word she'd use to describe what she was feeling for Dallas. Attraction? Sizzle? She felt those in spades. Neither seemed appropriate under the circumstances. But there was something about the strong cowboy that pulled her toward him. Something she'd never felt with another man. Not even with Robert. And she wasn't sure how to begin to process that. Kate had loved Robert…hadn't she?

She'd been married to the man and yet she hadn't felt this strong of a pull toward him. There was something about the cowboy that caused goose bumps on her arms every time he was near. So much more than sexual attraction.

And even in all the craziness, she couldn't ignore the heat of that kiss.

Chapter Six

To say the ranch was impressive was like saying Bill Gates had done okay for himself.

The land itself was stunning even though the cold front had stripped trees of their foliage, scattering orange and brown leaves across the front lawn.

The main building was especially striking. It was an imposing two stories with white siding and black shutters bracketing the windows. Grand white columns with orange and black ribbons adorned the expansive porch filled with black, orange and white pumpkins. Large pots of yellow and orange gerbera daisies led up the couple of stairs to the veranda, where pairs of white rocking chairs grouped together on both sides. The dark silhouette of a witch loomed in the top right window. Kate counted fourteen in all, including a set of French doors on the second floor complete with a quaint terrace. When she thought of a Texas ranch, this was exactly the kind of picture that would've come to mind.

The place was alive with charm and a very big part of her wished this for Jackson. Given the strain on her family since the divorce and the adoption, she didn't expect to go home for the holidays this year.

In fact, that was the last fight she and her mother had had.

If her mom couldn't support her decision and accept Jackson, then Kate had no intention of visiting at Halloween, Thanksgiving or anytime. Jackson was just as much a part of the family as she was, so rejecting him was no different than rejecting her.

Thinking about the fight still made her sad and she wished her mother understood. But her mom had been clear. Kate had been clear. And neither seemed ready to budge.

And right now, Kate had bigger problems than disagreeing with her mother over her adoption.

"Do you live here?" Kate asked, wiping away a sneaky tear while trying to take in all the warmth and grandeur of the place.

"I do now but not in this building. This was my parents' home. They opened up a wing for club guests and there are offices on the other side. My brothers and I each have our own hacienda at various places on the land," he said. "Our parents built them in hopes we'd stay on after college."

"Your parents don't live here anymore?" she asked, unable to imagine leaving such a beautiful home.

Dallas shook his head, and seeing the look on his face, a mix of sorrow and reverence, she regretted the question.

"They died a few weeks ago." He said the words

quietly, but the anguish in his voice nearly robbed her of breath.

She exhaled and said, "I'm so sorry."

He put the car in Park, cut the engine and stared out the front window for a few seconds. "Let's get some food in you," he finally said. Then he opened the door and exited the car.

Before she could get her seat belt off, Dallas was opening her door and holding out his hand. She was greeted by a chocolate Lab.

"Who's this guy?" she asked, patting him on the head.

"That's Denali. Been in the family fourteen years," Dallas said.

"He's beautiful." She took his outstretched hand, ignoring the sensual shivers vibrating up her arm from the point of contact. What could she say? Dallas was strong, handsome. The cowboy had shown up just in time to save her and her son from a terrible fate. So she couldn't deny a powerful attraction.

He was also a complete stranger, a little voice reminded her—a voice that repeated those words louder, a warning from the logical side of her brain.

Maybe if she had taken more time to get to know Robert before she'd jumped into a relationship and marriage, things might've turned out differently, that same annoying voice warned.

Instead, she'd allowed herself to be influenced by his easy charm and good looks. She'd gone against her better judgment after a couple of months of dating when he'd handed her a glass of wine and asked if she wanted to "get hitched and make babies."

Looking back, a piece of her, the logical side, had known all along that she didn't know Robert well enough to make a lifelong commitment. She'd been young and had given in to impulse.

And when things didn't go as planned, he'd bolted.

Not that she could really blame him for wanting out when she couldn't make the last part happen. He'd been clear that babies had been part of the deal all along. And his attention had wandered after that. Or maybe even before. Kate couldn't be sure. All she knew for certain was the information in the texts that she'd seen once she'd figured out he was having an affair. Even though she should've read the signs long before, and maybe a little part of her knew, there was still something about discovering proof of his lies—seeing them right there in front of her—that had knocked the wind out of her.

Logically, she knew all men were not Robert. But her heart, the part of her that withstood reason, knew she'd never be able to completely trust a man or a relationship again. She'd always question her judgment when it came to them now.

Dallas held the front door open for her as she forced her thoughts to the present. One step at a time, she entered the O'Brien home. The inside was even more breathtaking than the outside, if that was possible.

"Did you grow up here?" She imagined him and his brothers chasing each other up one side and down the other of the twin staircases in the foyer.

"Yes, ma'am," Dallas said, and there was something about his deep baritone that sent sensual shivers racing down her back.

"It must've been a wonderful childhood," she said and then chided herself for saying it out loud. She, of all people, should know that looks could be deceiving when it came to families. Maybe her perfect-on-the-outside relationship with Robert had been easy to fake, given that she'd grown up in a similar situation. Oh, the holiday cards her mother had insisted on posing for and sending out had painted a different picture. In those, they'd looked like the ideal family, complete with the requisite perfect boy and girl. What couldn't be seen in those paper faces and forced smiles was the constant bickering between her parents. Or how much her mom had needed both her children to be perfect in every way.

Kate could still see the disappointment in her mother's eyes when she'd brought home a C in Lit or when her SAT scores didn't quite measure up to expectations.

Their relationship had really started to fragment when Kate left for college and declared that she wanted to study computers instead of interior design. Her mom had thrown another fit, saying that career field was unfeminine.

Even when Kate and Carter had created a successful tech business together, their mother hadn't changed her position. She'd mostly been impressed with Carter and had insinuated that he'd carried Kate.

In selling her share, she'd done well enough to buy a house in Bluff, finance an adoption and provide the seed money to start The Food Project. And she'd still managed to save enough money for Jackson to study whatever he wanted in college.

"It was," Dallas said, bringing her out of her reverie. And she realized he'd been studying her reaction all along.

"So you spent your whole life here?" Kate asked, following him down the hall and into an impressive kitchen, the chocolate Lab at her heels.

There were batches of cookies in various stages of cooking. The place smelled like warmth and fall and everything wonderful. "Is that hot apple cider mulling on the stove?"

Dallas nodded and gave a half smile. "Janis goes all out this time of year through New Year's. She keeps this place running and has been helping my family most of my life. Would you like some cider?"

An older woman padded in from the hallway. "Dallas O'Brien, what are you doing in my kitchen this late? I expected you two hours ago for lunch," she said.

"Janis, I'd like you to meet Kate." He motioned toward her.

Janis wasn't tall, had to be right at five foot or a little more. She was round and grandmotherly with soft features.

Kate held out her hand. "Nice to meet you."

"My apologies for being so rude. I didn't realize Dallas had company," Janis said, shaking Kate's hand heartily. She had on a witch hat and her face was painted green.

Janis must've caught Kate's once-over because she

added, "And forgive this old outfit. I just delivered cookies to The Learning Bridge Preschool for Special Children."

"You look—"

"Silly to anyone standing over three feet tall," Janis said drolly, cutting Kate off.

"I was going to say 'as adorable as a witch.'"

The woman grinned from ear to ear.

Kate wasn't trying to score brownie points with the comment, but it seemed that she had.

"Well, then, can I get you something to eat? I made a special Italian sausage soup this morning," Janis said. "Can't believe how cold it is this early in the season. Then again, I shouldn't be surprised given how unpredictable Texas weather can be."

"That sounds like heaven." Kate smiled. She couldn't help but like pretty much everything about the O'Brien house. She could imagine the look on Jackson's face when he was older, running through halls like these, surrounded by family.

Her heart squeezed, because Jackson would never have that. But he had her and Carter, and they would have to be enough, she told herself. Or maybe just her, that irritating little voice said, because Carter hadn't been out to meet his nephew yet, either.

"There's a formal eating space in the other room, but this is where my brothers and I prefer to hang out." Dallas motioned toward the oversize wood table in the kitchen. "Janis would tease us and say it's because we weren't taught enough manners to sit in the other room."

"This is perfect. Closer to the source," Kate said.

"Where is everybody?" Dallas inquired.

"After lunch, they all took off outside. A few of the boys headed to the barn. Austin said he would be running fences if anyone needed him," Janis added, bringing two steaming bowls of soup to the table.

"He's been doing that a lot lately," Dallas noted thoughtfully, almost as if talking to himself. "I'll check on him later." He walked over to the stove.

"Running fences?" Kate asked.

"We have livestock on the property, so every foot of fence has to be routinely checked," he explained.

The hearty soup smelled amazing and Kate figured it was about the only thing she would be able to get down. Even though she knew she should eat, it was the last thing on her mind, since her nerves were fried and her stomach was tied in knots.

Dallas brought her a cup of apple cider and it smelled even more delicious. But nothing was as appealing as Dallas when he hesitated near her. His scent was a powerful mix of virile male and the great outdoors, and it affected her in ways she didn't want to think about right then.

"This food is amazing." She couldn't allow herself to get too carried away in the moment because the horrible events of the day were constant in her thoughts, and being separated from Jackson even though he was safe at the sheriff's office was another reminder of their present danger. Her son being secure was the most important thing, and she needed to get back to him as soon as possible.

The best way to do that would be to figure out what was going on and stop it, she reminded herself.

"Janis is the best cook in Collier County," Dallas was saying, and the older woman smiled.

"Did you make contact with Stacy to let her know we're coming?" Kate asked a moment later, focusing on the problem at hand.

"I'll do that now." Dallas took a seat across the table from her, fished his phone from his front pocket and then sent a text.

The soup tasted every bit as good as it smelled and eased her queasy stomach instantly.

Janis brought over a plate of fresh bread before asking Dallas to keep an eye on the timer for the latest batch of cookies while she changed into regular clothes.

"Earlier, you gave the impression you'd moved back to the ranch. Where did you live before?" Kate asked him.

"I had a logistics business based in New Mexico," he explained.

"I've been to Taos to ski," she offered.

"Up the mountain is too cold for my blood." Dallas laughed and the sound of his voice filled the room. "But then, I figure you know a thing or two about that, given the way you were dressed this morning."

"There's no substitute for sunshine and Texas summers," Kate said. "Why did you move back?"

"THERE WERE A lot of reasons to come home, but the main one was to run the ranch with my brothers," Dallas said. His business in New Mexico was booming and he'd built a life there, but no sacrifice was too great for his family, and he'd always known that he'd return to the ranch full-time at some point. This land was where his heart belonged.

"I'm sorry again about your parents." Kate must've realized the real reason he'd returned.

"We inherited the place along with an aunt and uncle, and I guess it just felt right to keep ownership in the family. Between the cattle ranch and rifle club, this place is more than a full-time job and it takes all of us pitching in to keep it going. Especially now. We're still getting our arms around the business, while a few of us are in the process of selling off our other interests."

"How many brothers did you say you have?" Kate asked, taking another spoonful of soup. The little moan of pleasure in her throat made him think of their kiss— a kiss that wasn't far from his thoughts, no matter how little business it had being there.

"Five, so there are six of us total. One is still living in Colorado, but the others are settling their affairs and/or living here. The youngest two are twins," he said. Dallas wasn't much of a talker usually, but conversation with Kate came easy.

"Twins?" she gasped. "My hands are full with one baby."

Dallas couldn't hold back a chuckle. "Tommy practically grew up in this house, too. He came to live with his uncle, Chill Johnson, who's been a ranch hand since longer than I can remember. So he makes a solid seven boys."

The bewildered look in Kate's eyes was amusing. "I can't even imagine having that many kids around. Taking care of Jackson is keeping me busier than I ever thought possible." She glanced about. "Then again, it's just me and Jackson."

Something flashed in her eyes that Dallas couldn't quite put his finger on.

"Despite having plenty of help around, Mom insisted on taking care of us herself," he said. "She was an original DIY type."

"Then she really was an amazing woman," Kate declared.

"Pop helped out a lot," Dallas added. "Being the oldest, so did I. They were forced to hire more help around the ranch, especially as they got older and we moved on to make our own way in life."

The look of admiration in Kate's eyes shouldn't make Dallas feel proud. But he didn't want to spend any more time talking about himself.

He wanted to learn more about Kate Williams.

Before he could ask a question, she'd devoured the contents of her bowl, drained her cider and made a move to stand.

"We should head to your detective agency," she said, and that look of determination was back. That was most likely a good thing, because Dallas didn't need to go down that path, didn't need to go to the place where he was getting to know her better and learning about all the little ticks that made her unique. Especially if Susan's baby turned out to be Jackson.

As he walked her to the front door, Janis met them in the hallway.

"I almost forgot to tell you that your uncle Ezra was around looking for you this morning," she said. "He and his sister are at it again, and I think Ezra was jockeying for support. He said that he didn't want to trouble you, but when one of your brothers shot down his idea he felt he needed to get another opinion."

"If he's still angling to get an invite for the McCabe family to the bash then he's barking up the wrong tree." Hollister McCabe and Dallas's father had been at odds for years. McCabe had been trying to buy fifty acres from Pop, and when Dallas's dad had refused, the other rancher had tried to strong-arm a local politician to force the issue. That hadn't gone over well with the self-made, independent-minded senior O'Brien.

And Dallas had never trusted the McCabe family. Especially since Faith McCabe was one of Susan's best friends. That should've been enough of a red flag for him. Maybe it was the fact that he'd missed home that had drawn him to date Susan in the first place. Susan had always loved Bluff, so it was even more of a surprise that she'd come to New Mexico. Tommy had balked when Dallas had told his friend about who had shown up to a job interview at D.O. Logistics, the successful company Dallas had founded. He'd said that he shouldn't be too surprised given how much she'd been talking about missing Dallas around town.

"I believe that was one of Ezra's complaints," Janis

said, snapping his mind to the current conversation. "But he's always got something up his sleeve."

Knowing Ezra, that was the tip of the iceberg. He'd been making a play for more control over the family business since before Pop's death—a business Pop had begun and made a success on his own. In the weeks since his death, Ezra's efforts had doubled.

Pop had included his siblings, giving them a combined 5 percent of the company in order to help them be more independent in their older years. Pop was a tough businessman, but his heart was gold, and even though he'd disagreed with his brother and sister on most counts, he'd felt a responsibility to take care of family.

Dallas could relate to the emotion, being the oldest of the O'Brien siblings, and was grateful that his brothers shared the same work ethic as he did and he wouldn't have to carry them.

"Gearing up for the holiday season always brings out the best in those two, doesn't it," he said to Janis, shaking his head.

"I don't know why they have to act up around the biggest parties of the year." She nodded and took in a slow breath.

"How's planning going for the Halloween Bash?" Dallas asked.

"Good. Busy. You know how it is around this time. You'd think with all we have going on that he'd relax." She paused and then added, "But no. He's always scheming. Families can be *interesting* sometimes."

"That's a good word for it," Dallas agreed. Janis

had become as much a part of the O'Brien clan as anyone in her decades of service.

"Will you be back in time for supper?" she asked.

"Not exactly sure. Don't hold it up on my account, though. Also, I need to let the others know I have a situation to deal with and I might need their assistance. Do you mind helping with that?" Dallas asked.

"Consider it done."

"Hold on." He moved to his father's gun cabinet and pulled out his favorite, a .25 caliber, put on a shoulder holster and secured the weapon underneath his coat.

He returned, thanked Janis and then placed his hand on the small of Kate's back to usher her out the front door. It was too much to ignore the heat rippling through him from the contact, even though she wore a coat, so he accepted it.

There was no use denying the fact that Kate was a beautiful woman. Dallas needed to leave it at that. Because not keeping his feelings in check would just complicate an already crazy situation. Hormones had no place in the equation. He'd already decided to offer her and Jackson a place to stay on the ranch. There was plenty of room in his hacienda, and Tommy would be hard-pressed to find anywhere for them with better security.

And Dallas didn't need to create an unnecessary distraction because of the feelings he was developing for Kate. *Feelings? This soon?*

He wasn't going to touch that one.

Besides, having her and the baby stay with him had everything to do with offering a safe place for the mother and child. State-of-the-art security was a necessity on the ranch, given that this part of south-central Texas was known for poachers. Other than being some of the worst scum on earth, poachers presented a danger to their clients and the hunting expeditions offered by the Cattlemen Crime Club.

KATE WAS QUIET on the ride over. Dallas exited the sedan and she followed suit. He'd caught a glimpse of her, of the questions she had. At least for now she seemed to think better of asking.

"Mr. O'Brien, how can I help you?" Stacy peeked out the door. The petite brunette wore business attire that highlighted her curves. Based on her puffy eyes, Dallas guessed she'd been crying all day.

"I'm here to talk to you about Wayne and the case he was investigating," Dallas said.

"Of course you are. Come in. I'm sorry. My mind's not right. Not since learning about Wayne this morning from the deputy." She froze, embarrassment crossing her features, and then corrected herself. "Mr. Morton. It's all such a shock."

Based on the woman's general demeanor, it occurred to Dallas that she and Morton might have had more than a working relationship. Given the circumstances, he wasn't surprised that she looked in such bad shape.

"This is my friend Kate Williams," Dallas said.

"Please, come in," Stacy said. "It's nice to meet you."

She and Kate shook hands as she invited them inside.

"Has anyone else been here to speak to you?" Dallas asked, instinctively positioning himself between Kate and the door.

"Just the appointments Wayne—Mr. Morton— already had on the books," Stacy said, blowing her nose into a wrinkled handkerchief. "Excuse me. I'm sorry, but I'm just a mess. He was a good guy, you know, and I can't believe he's gone."

"No need to apologize," Dallas said quickly, guilt settling on his shoulders yet again. He knew full well that Morton would still be alive were it not for Safe Haven and Dallas's case. "I couldn't be sorrier this happened."

"It's not like his job doesn't bring with it a certain amount of danger," she continued, as more tears rolled down her cheeks. "He's licensed to carry."

Dallas knew that meant Morton had been armed.

"And he went to the gun range all the time to keep his skills sharp," she said with a hiccup. "I just can't believe someone would get to him first like that."

"It shouldn't have happened. Other than working on my case, has there been anything unusual going on lately with Wayne? Has he been keeping any late nights or other appointments off the books?" Dallas asked, knowing Safe Haven was the reason Morton was dead, but wishing for another explanation.

"No. Not that I can think of, anyway, but then, you know Wayne." She seemed to drop the front of being strictly professional with her boss. "He took on extra assignments all the time, which didn't mean I'd know about them."

Any hope, however small, that this wasn't Dallas's fault was slowly dying.

More tears spilled out of Stacy's eyes and she looked like she needed to sit down.

Dallas urged her toward one of the seats in the lounge area of Morton's expansive office. She perched on the arm of a leather chair as Kate took a seat near her on the matching sofa.

"First of all, I want to say that I'm really sorry about Wayne," Kate said sympathetically, leaning toward her. "I can only imagine the pain you must be feeling right now."

The gesture must've created an intimacy between the two because Stacy leaned forward, too, and her tense shoulders relaxed a bit.

"I just keep expecting him to walk through that door," she said, looking away. "It hasn't really hit yet that he's not going to, ever again."

"It's unfair to have something unthinkable happen to someone you love," Kate continued. "My son was almost abducted this morning and we're here because we think the cases might be connected."

Kate was taking a long shot, but Dallas understood why she'd need to try.

"Where are my manners?" the other woman asked, looking noticeably uncomfortable. "Can I get either of you something to drink?"

"No, thank you," Kate said.

"Can you tell me what's been going on the past few days? Maybe a timeline of his activities would help," Dallas said.

"He's been acting weird ever since he started investigating that adoption agency for—" Stacy glanced from Dallas to Kate "—you."

"How long ago did he fit the pieces together of Susan and Safe Haven?" he asked, as Kate crossed her legs and folded her arms. Everything about her body language said she was closing up on him.

He shouldn't be surprised. They knew very little about each other aside from facts pertaining to her case. Circumstances had thrown them together and they'd been through more this morning than most people would in a year. There was an undeniable pull, an attraction, between them, but that was where it ended. Where it had to end. As soon as she and Jackson were safe, Kate and Dallas would return to their respective lives.

"Let's see…" Stacy leaned back and thrummed her manicured fingernails on her thigh. "It had to be recently, because he decided to make an official visit this morning and he never does that before he thoroughly checks out a place. Normally, he gives me names—" she paused long enough to glance between Kate and Dallas "—just in case things go sour. This time, he only gave me the address where he was going. He didn't even tell me the name of the agency. I had to look it up on the internet when he didn't come home after checking the place out last night. Then I called the sheriff's office and spoke to a deputy. Not long after, they found his car."

Dallas figured all the secrecy was due to the fact he'd paid Morton extra in order to keep the information private. The last thing Dallas needed was for a news outlet to get wind of what was going on. Not that he gave a damn about his own reputation. People had a way of making up their own minds with or without actual facts. He was trying to keep Susan's name out of the papers, as well as that of the family business. The amount of false leads news like this could generate would make it next to impossible for Tommy to sort out fact from fiction and would add too much weight to the investigation. A whole lot of people would likely come out of the woodwork to get their hands on O'Brien money if they thought a reward was involved.

"Any idea about the trail leading up to Safe Haven? Who Wayne might have contacted in order to get that information in the first place?" Dallas asked, hoping for a miracle.

"Those are great questions," Stacy said, looking flustered. "He usually runs everything past me, but he was keeping this one close to the vest. He does that with special clients, so I didn't think to ask more. Believe me, I've been kicking myself all day over it."

"You couldn't have known this would happen," Kate said sympathetically.

The woman smiled weakly.

"Does he keep a file on his more discreet clients in the office anywhere?" Dallas pressed. Tommy wouldn't like that he had asked the question, but this was starting to feel like a complete dead end. For the sheriff to get the records, he'd have to get a court order, which would take time. Dallas didn't have that luxury. He had a woman and child being targeted, no answers, and his own personal agenda to explore. If investigating Safe Haven was responsible for Morton's murder, then they could also be the reason Susan hadn't turned up.

Dallas was still trying to figure out why the kidnappers would change their MO, using a knife instead of a gun when they'd targeted Jackson. If it was the same group, that didn't make sense.

Stacy was too distraught to think clearly, which was understandable under the circumstances.

And now Kate had locked up on him, too.

Dallas was cursing under his breath just as the door to Morton's office flew open and two men burst in.

Stacy jumped to her feet and ran toward them, blocking Dallas's view. "The office is closed. You need an appointment to come in here."

The entrance to the private bathroom was about six steps away. If he could get Kate inside and lock the door, then he could face down the pair of men threatening Stacy.

Just as Dallas made it to the door, Stacy shouted, *"Go!"*

Chapter Seven

Before Dallas could react, a bullet cracked through the air, and a split second later Stacy let out a yelp. Another bullet pinged into the wood not a foot from Dallas's head. He ducked and shoved Kate into the bathroom, falling on top of her. He performed a quick check to see if either one of them had been hit, needing to get her to safety so he could return to Stacy.

The guys in the other room had no intention of allowing him or Kate to walk out of here alive. They hadn't come for Stacy, so her best chance at survival was if he and Kate got the hell out of Dodge.

Dallas closed and locked the door.

The office was on the second floor, which could present a problem getting out the window. Land the wrong way, break an ankle and it was game over.

"Where is he?" one of the men asked.

"I don't see him," the other replied.

The first man cursed.

As Dallas moved to the small box window, he quickly scanned himself and Kate again for signs of blood, relieved when he saw none. From his experience with guns, he knew that bullets didn't travel in a straight line. They rose after exiting the barrel and then started dropping. Aiming a fraction of an inch off could make a decent marksman miss his target even at fairly close range.

Dallas opened the window and checked below. A row of bushes would help break Kate's fall.

He stepped aside, allowing her enough room to climb into the small space. She'd fit through it just fine, but Dallas was much bulkier. He'd have a difficult time getting through that tiny opening.

"Take your coat off," he said.

She pushed it through the window and let it drop to the ground.

"Run as soon as you get down there. Don't wait for me, okay?" he said, boosting her up to the window ledge.

She hesitated, which meant she must've realized what he already knew—he'd be trapped if he couldn't squeeze through. He knew she was about to put up an argument. He couldn't let her. She had a child depending on her and she had to make it to safety.

So he hoisted her up and through before she could protest, hoping that she'd call Tommy as soon as she was in the clear.

On closer inspection, the window was definitely too small for him to climb through, so he decided to create a diversion to keep the men engaged upstairs while Kate escaped.

The knob jiggled and then it sounded like someone was taking a hammer to the door followed by a male-sounding grunt.

"We're coming out. Get down on the floor," he

shouted, pulling the .25 caliber from his holster. He fired a shot at the panel.

A few bullets pinged around him, so he dropped to the tiles. Scuffling noises in the other room gave him the impression the guys might be leaving. That couldn't be good. Then again, it could be a ploy to draw him out.

"Stacy," he shouted and then quickly changed position so they couldn't target him based on his voice.

Dallas palmed his phone and dialed 911. He immediately requested police and an ambulance and then ended the call.

Next, he moved to the window to check on Kate. His chest almost went into spasm as he realized what could've happened to her. He pushed his head through the opening and scanned the row of boxwoods below, releasing a relieved breath when he didn't see her.

Surveying the area between buildings revealed no signs of her, either.

Good.

He'd have to take a risk in order to check on Stacy. She might be hurt and there was no way he'd leave her bleeding out when he could help.

Dallas listened at the door for what felt an eternity, but was more likely a minute. There were no sounds coming from the other room. He muttered a string of swearwords, took a deep breath and then opened the door a crack.

He couldn't get a visual on anyone, so he opened the door a little more.

Footsteps shuffled on the wooden stairs leading down to the street.

As soon as he realized the men were gone, Dallas bolted toward Stacy, who was on the floor curled in a ball. Not moving.

"Stacy." He repeated her name as he dropped to his knees beside her. Red soaked her shirt by her right shoulder. He felt for a pulse and got one.

"Hang in there, Stacy," he said. "Help is on the way."

Dallas could already hear sirens, and relief washed over him when her eyes fluttered open.

More footsteps sounded, growing louder. Could the men be returning to finish the job with Dallas?

They'd been looking for someone. A man?

He pointed his gun at the door, with every intention of firing on anyone who walked through it. He couldn't leave Stacy alone, especially when she gripped his hand. He was her lifeline right now and he knew it.

The door burst open as Dallas's finger hovered over the trigger, ready to fire.

"Dallas," Kate said, her chest heaving from running. "Oh, my gosh. Is she okay?"

"Get inside and shut the door behind you," Dallas growled, lowering his pistol. He knew the door locked from prior visits to Morton's office. "Shove the back of that chair against the knob. Let only the law or an EMT cross that threshold."

Kate did.

Dallas cradled the wounded woman's head and

neck in his free hand. "Stay with me, Stacy," he said. "Help is almost here."

"I loved him," she said, and the words were difficult to make out.

"I know you did. And he loved you, too," Dallas replied, trying to comfort her. He was never more thankful than when an emergency team showed up and went to work on her.

The gunshot wound in her shoulder was deep and she'd lost a lot of blood. As the EMT strapped her to a gurney and another placed an oxygen mask over her nose and mouth, Dallas heard them reassure her that she was going to be fine.

And Dallas finally exhaled. He palmed his phone and called Tommy with a quick explanation of what had just gone down.

The lawman agreed to take their statements personally and said he'd let the deputy who was about to arrive on the scene know the details. "Do not visit Safe Haven."

Dallas contemplated his friend's suggestion. Tommy was right. "I won't. I'm bringing Kate to the station."

"Good," Tommy said, ending the call.

"Let's get out of here," Dallas said to Kate.

She didn't utter a word as they made their way back to her vehicle, and he suspected she was in shock.

"I'm driving to my truck first," he stated, as he fired up the engine. "And then I'm going to drop you off at the sheriff's office, where you'll be safe."

"That was horrible," Kate murmured, obviously

still stunned and trying to process everything that had just happened.

"I'm sorry. I shouldn't have brought you here." Dallas half expected her to curse him out for putting her in danger.

"It's not your fault, and I can't go back to the station until we figure this out," she said. "So where are we heading next?"

"We have no idea where those men could be or why they left," he said. "You're going back to the sheriff's office."

Gripping the steering wheel, Dallas noticed the blood on his hands. Anger surged through him that he hadn't been able to stop Stacy from being shot. No way would he put Kate in further danger. She could argue all she wanted, but he was taking her back to Tommy.

Then Dallas had to fill his brothers in on the situation, so he could hide her at the ranch.

He had every intention of helping Kate and Jackson, so he needed to have a family meeting to figure out how best to proceed. It wouldn't be fair to put at risk anyone who wasn't comfortable with that.

And Dallas might have a target on his own back now that he'd stirred up an investigation into Safe Haven. That would bring more heat to the ranch—heat that he had no doubt they'd be able to handle.

His cell buzzed. Dallas took one hand off the wheel to fish it out of his pocket.

"Would you mind answering that and putting the call on speaker?" He handed his phone to Kate.

She took it and did as he asked.

"This is Dallas and you're on speaker with me and Kate," he said.

"Where are you?" Tommy asked, and Dallas immediately picked up on the underlying panic in his friend's calm tone.

"Heading toward Main to get my pickup. Why?" Dallas asked, an ominous feeling settling over him.

"Someone just tried to break into my office," the sheriff said. "Jackson is okay. He didn't get to him."

Kate gasped. Dallas didn't need to look at her to know her eyes were wild, just like they'd been earlier that morning.

"What happened?" he asked, glancing at her before making the next left. His pickup could wait. Based on Kate's tense expression, she needed to get to her son and see for herself that he wasn't harmed.

"He's safe," Tommy reiterated. "I have him in protective custody and I promise no one will get to him on my watch."

The desperate look Kate gave Dallas sent a lead fireball swirling through him.

"WE'RE ON OUR WAY," Dallas said. "Did you find anything at the Morton crime scene?"

"Nothing yet. It'll take a while to process and it could be days or weeks before we get anything back from analysis," Tommy said truthfully.

Kate had had so many other questions—questions about the man sitting in the driver's seat beside her—

all of which died on her tongue the second she'd heard that Jackson was in danger.

Dallas couldn't drive fast enough to get her to the station so she could see her son. Her brain was spinning and her heart beat furiously, but more than anything her body ached to hold her baby.

Dallas thanked the sheriff and asked her to end the call.

Whoever was after them had proved at Morton's office just how dangerous they could be. People were being shot right before her eyes, not to mention turning up dead. She and Dallas had barely survived another blitz-like attack, this time with guns.

The thought of men like that being after her baby was almost too much to process at once. It was surreal.

She remembered them asking if "he" was there. Did they mean Jackson? If so, they must've realized he wasn't with her.

Nothing could happen to her little boy. He was more than her son; he'd been her heart from the moment the adoption liaison had placed him in her arms. The thought of anyone trying to take him away from her, especially after how hard she'd fought to get him, was enough to boil her blood.

"Why would they want to harm an innocent little baby?" she fumed.

"They don't. I know how bad things look right now, but even if they got to Jackson, and they won't, they wouldn't hurt him."

"How can you be so sure? People are being shot, killed," she countered.

"Think about it. Hurting him doesn't make sense. A few of the other babies have been returned. My guess is that someone is looking for their child, a child they very much want," Dallas said.

He was right.

Logic was beginning to take hold.

And yet that didn't stop her blood from scorching.

"A stray bullet could've killed him," she said.

Dallas agreed.

"How much longer until we get there?" She didn't recognize any of the streets yet. Not that she'd been anywhere aside from home and downtown at the soup kitchen in the six months she'd been in Bluff. There had been a couple of donor parties, but most of them were lined up in the future. The Halloween Bash at the ranch that she'd been invited to was next on the agenda, but the last thing she could think about was a party.

"I'm taking a back road, so I can make sure we aren't being followed, and because this should shave off a few minutes." He floored the gas pedal, pushing her car to its limit. "We'll be there in five."

"I'm scared," she said, hating how weak her voice sounded.

"I know," he murmured—all he had to say to make her feel she wasn't alone. "Jackson is in good hands."

"They tried to…"

She couldn't finish, couldn't face the harsh reality that someone was this determined to find her son and take him away from her.

"We know whoever is behind this is capable of horrendous acts," Dallas said. "But they wouldn't hurt Jackson even if they could get to him, which they can't and they won't."

"You said it before and you're right," she admitted, and it brought a little relief. Still, the idea that Jackson could be taken away and she might never see him again, when he was the very thing that had breathed life into her, was unthinkable.

Kate might not have been deemed "medically desirable" by nature—wasn't that the phrase the infertility specialist had used?—but she was born to be a mother. She'd stayed awake the entire first night with Jackson while he'd slept in her arms. And it hadn't mattered to her heart one bit that she hadn't been the one to deliver him—Jackson was her son in every way that mattered.

Being a mother was the greatest joy.

And no one—no one—got to take that away from her.

Dallas pulled into the parking lot of the sheriff's office. His set jaw said he was on a mission, too. And it was so nice that someone had her back for a change. Carter had been her lifeline before, but even he'd had his doubts about her plans, and she never saw her brother since leaving the business.

She also knew that Dallas had questions of his own

about Safe Haven. Supposedly for a friend but she wondered if that was true. No matter how many times she'd thought about the kiss they'd shared this morning, she was keenly aware of the fact that this man had secrets.

As soon as the car stopped, Kate unbuckled her seat belt.

"Hold on there," Dallas warned. "Someone might be waiting out here."

That could very well be true, but she was determined to see her son.

She practically flew through the door, Dallas was a step behind, and all eyes jumped to her.

"I'm sorry." She held up a hand. "I didn't mean to startle anyone. I'm looking for my son."

At that moment, she heard Jackson cry from somewhere down the hall and she moved toward the sweet sound of her baby.

Abigail met her halfway and handed Jackson over, and then Dallas was suddenly by her side, just as Tommy appeared from his office.

"Hold on. I need to call my brothers," he said, stepping inside a room while digging out his cell.

He returned a few minutes later with a nod.

"I need to get him out of here," Kate said. "And to someplace safe."

"You can't take him home." The sheriff didn't sound like he was disagreeing so much as ruling out possibilities.

"She can take him to my place," Dallas said. "I

just had a quick conversation with my brothers about it. They don't have a problem with the arrangement."

Tommy looked to be seriously contemplating the idea.

"I don't want to put your family at risk," Kate argued.

"I can put you in a safe house but it might take a little time," the lawman said. "You'd be welcome to stay here in the office in the meantime."

"My place is better," Dallas protested as he shifted his weight. "You already know how tight security is."

"I advised you on every aspect of it," Tommy agreed. "But—"

Dallas's hand came up. "It's perfect and you know it. There's no safer place in Bluff right now. My family is fine with the risk."

Kate hesitated, trying to think if she had another option. She could go to her brother's house, but it was nearly a four-hour drive and he had no security. Also, she might be placing him in danger. Ditto for her parents' home. She couldn't risk her family, and honestly, she'd have so much explaining to do it wasn't worth the effort.

No, if these guys were bold enough to strike at the sheriff's office, then they would stop at nothing to get to Jackson.

At least for now, she had no other options but to stay with Dallas until a proper safe house could be set up. Jackson's security was the most important thing to her and had to take precedence over her internal battle about whether or not spending time with the strong and secretive cowboy was a good idea for her personally.

"I'm all for any place we can keep Jackson safe," she said to the sheriff. "If you think this is a good idea."

Tommy nodded.

"Then let's go back to the ranch," she said.

The sheriff shot a look toward Dallas that Kate couldn't get a good read on. What was up with that?

She didn't care. The only thing she was focused on at this point was her son. And ensuring that he didn't end up in the hands of very bad men. She held him tighter to her chest and he quieted at the sound of her voice as she whispered comforting words.

"Allen can go now, right?" she asked Tommy. "If the attacks are still happening while he's locked up, then he can't be involved."

"A deputy is already processing his paperwork," the sheriff said.

"It's been a very long day and I'd like to get out of here," she said to Dallas. Then she turned toward Tommy. "Are you okay with us leaving?"

"Go. Get some rest. We're trying to track down your lawyer to bring him in for questioning. So far, he isn't answering our calls." Tommy paused. "Also, you should know that we're planning to send a deputy to talk to your family members."

"My family?" she echoed, not able to hide her shock.

"It's routine in cases like this," he said. "We take the 'no stone left unturned' approach to investigations."

Oh. Kate tried to process that, but it was all too much and she was experiencing information overload. She needed a few quiet hours to focus on feeding Jackson and allow everything that had happened that day to sink in. Even though it was only four o'clock in the afternoon, she was exhausted. A warm shower and comfortable pajamas sounded like pure heaven to her right then.

"And it might be better if they don't know we're coming," Tommy said, and the implication hit her square in the chest.

"Surely you don't think…" No way could her family be involved. She held on to Jackson tighter. They had their differences about the adoption, but they were still family.

"I won't take anything for granted," the lawman said.

Dallas's strong hand closed around her bent elbow, sending all kinds of heat through her arm. Heat that had no business fizzing through her body and settling between her thighs.

Dallas O'Brien was a complete stranger, and since that scenario had worked out so well the first time she'd broken her rules for someone, she decided no amount of chemistry was worth falling down another rabbit hole like that. But she wasn't fool enough to refuse his help.

He urged her toward the door and then to the car, surveying the area as they walked out.

She buckled Jackson into his seat and slid next to him in the back.

A few seconds later they were on the road again,

but this time Dallas drove the speed limit and she appreciated the extra care he was taking with her son in the car.

If Dallas O'Brien was a father, and she figured that had to be the real reason he was investigating Safe Haven, then he was going to be a great one. He already had all the protective instincts down.

She could only imagine what horrible circumstance had brought him the need to hire a private investigator, but decided not to let her imagination run wild. Especially when she kept circling back to that kiss and the fizz of chemistry that continued to crackle between them.

Because another thought quickly followed. How could a man who obviously loved his family so much allow his own child to be adopted? The question helped her see how precious little she knew about the magnetic cowboy. And even if she could risk the attraction on her own behalf, she'd never be able to go down that road now that she had a baby.

"Is there anything Tommy should know about your family?" Dallas asked, his voice a low rumble that set butterflies free in her stomach.

"You already know they don't support my decision to bring up a child alone," she said softly. "Our relationship has been strained since my divorce, and my mother sees *this*—" she motioned toward Jackson "—as me adding insult to injury."

In the rearview mirror, she could see Dallas's eyebrows spike. She could also see how his thick dark eyelashes framed his dark brown eyes, and her heart stirred in a way she'd never experienced.

She ignored that, too.

Besides, they'd dodged bullets and he'd saved her son. Of course she'd feel a certain amount of admiration and respect because of that, and a draw to his strength. That was normal in such a situation, right?

"I'm sorry about your folks. Everyone should have love and support from their family, even if they don't agree with your choices."

"My mom has never been the type to give up that kind of control," Kate said, trying to make a joke, but recognizing that the words came out carrying the pain she felt instead. "Sorry—you don't want to hear about this."

"I do," Dallas said so quickly she thought he meant it.

Why would he care about her family drama?

Kate didn't talk about it with anyone. She figured she'd have to explain to Jackson one day why he didn't have grandparents, but life for her was a "take one day at a time" commitment at the moment.

"That must be hard," Dallas said.

And lonely, she added in her head. Thank the stars for the relationship she had with Carter, barren as it was now that she didn't see him on a daily basis.

Speaking of which, she needed to call her brother as soon as Tommy gave her clearance.

Carter and she had forged a tight bond that had felt strained since Kate had said she was leaving the business they'd started. He had said he understood, but she knew down deep he'd been hurt by her decision.

"My brother and I were close growing up, and that helped," she said, trying to gain control of her emotions before she started crying. Even though she knew that her mother's rejection wasn't her fault, it still stung.

"Brothers can be a blessing and a curse," Dallas said, sounding like he was half joking.

She was grateful he seemed to take the cue that she needed a lighter mood. There was so much going on around them and she felt so out of control that she needed levity to help her get a handle on her emotions.

"That's the truth," she agreed, thinking about all those times her younger brother had annoyed her over the years.

She glanced down at Jackson. He was her sanity in this crazy, mixed-up world. He made her see that life was bigger than just her and her problems.

"I used to be so angry at my parents," she said, finding love refilling her well, as it did every time she looked at her son.

"What changed?"

"Him."

The surprised look on Dallas's face caught her off guard. Because there was something else there in his expression. It was so familiar and yet she couldn't quite put it into words. "Can I ask a personal question?" Kate murmured.

He nodded.

"Was Susan your girlfriend?"

"Yes. A while back," he admitted. He took a hard right turn and there was a security gate with a guard.

"And the baby you're investigating… Is that for you or a friend?" Kate didn't look at him.

"Me," he said so quietly that she almost didn't hear him.

"Where are we?" she asked, not recognizing the wooded area. Hadn't there been another layer of security earlier?

"This is the west end of the ranch property," he answered, as he was waved in by security.

When Dallas had told her he owned a hacienda on the ranch, she wasn't sure what she'd expected. A large shed? A tiny log cabin?

Certainly not this.

The gorgeous Spanish-style architecture was about the last thing she would have imagined.

He'd explained that each of his brothers had a place on various sites on the land. His sat near the west end so he could take advantage of the sunset.

"This whole property must be enormous," she said, eyes wide.

"Pop added acreage over the years," Dallas said as he parked in the three-car garage.

There was a vintage El Camino, completely restored, in the second.

"That belong to you, as well?" She hadn't thought about the fact that Dallas might not live alone.

"I like to work on cars in my spare time," he said, holding her door open. "That is, I did when I *used* to have free time."

She let him take the diaper bag as she unhooked Jackson, and then she followed Dallas into the house.

The kitchen was massive and had all gourmet appliances. There was an island in the center with enough room for four bar chairs.

"Is the ranch keeping you too busy to pursue your hobbies?" she asked.

"That and trying to transition my old business to the new owner," he said.

"Why sell? Why not hire someone to run the other business for you and keep it?" she asked.

"Didn't think I could do justice to either place that way." Dallas's tone was matter-of-fact. "If I'm involved in something then that's what I want to be able to put all my attention into, and not just write my name on an office door for show. A man's name, his reputation and his word are all he really has in life."

"Powerful thought," she said, trying not to admire this handsome stranger any more than she already did. Those were the kinds of principles she hoped to instill in her son.

Dallas stood there, his gaze meeting hers, and it felt like the world stopped for just that brief moment.

And that was dangerous.

Kate threw her shoulders back. "Is there somewhere I can give Jackson a bath?"

"Let me give you a quick tour so you'll know where everything is," he said. "My brothers arranged for you to have supplies waiting."

She nodded, afraid to speak. Afraid her voice would give away her emotions.

The rest of the house's decor was simple, clean and comfortable looking.

"A crib was delivered from the main house. They keep a few on hand up there for overnight guests." He stopped in the middle of the living room. "If you need to reach out to your employees, I'd rather not alert anyone to the fact that you're here. The fewer people who know where you and Jackson are, the better."

"I know I already asked, but are you sure this is a good idea?"

"The security staff knows we have a special guest and that you're staying at my place. They'll tell maintenance what they need to know to stay safe, so no one's in the dark. But it'll be best to keep your identity as quiet as possible," Dallas said, showing her the bathroom attached to her guest suite. "Is there anything else I can do?"

"Once I'm able to put Jackson down, I'd love clean clothes to change into after a hot shower."

A dark shadow passed through Dallas's eyes.

"What's wrong?"

"I don't want to think about you naked in the shower," he grumbled. Then he said something about making a fresh pot of coffee and walked out of the room.

Kate smiled in spite of herself. She didn't want to like the handsome cowboy any more than she already did. Her heart still hadn't recovered from its last disappointment.

And an attraction like the one she felt for the cowboy could be far more threatening than anything she'd experienced with Robert.

Adding to her confusion was the fact that Dallas O'Brien had secrets.

Chapter Eight

He had tried not to watch too intently as Kate fed Jackson his bottle. But Dallas couldn't help his natural curiosity now that the seal had been broken on that subject and the possibility he was a father grew a fraction of an inch.

"Mind keeping an eye on him while I clean up?" Kate asked and then laughed at Dallas's startled reaction.

Dallas couldn't say he'd had a stunning track record watching his brothers. Colin had broken his arm twice in one year on the tire swing Pop had set up on the old oak in the yard. Both the twins, Ryder and Joshua, had endured broken bones more than once on Dallas's watch, while climbing trees, and then there was the time Tyler had rolled around in poison ivy. And forget about Austin. That kid had had Pop joking that he needed a physician on staff for all the sprained ankles and banged-up body parts over the years.

"You sure about this? I'm not exactly qualified to take care of a baby," Dallas said, eyeing the sleeping infant.

The little boy looked so peaceful and innocent.

And Dallas figured that would last until Kate turned on the water in the shower.

"I think you'll be okay while he's out. He's a heavy sleeper," she said. "Or I could just take him in the bathroom with me and open the shower curtain to keep an eye on him, if you're not comfortable."

"No, don't do that," Dallas said, figuring he might need to know how to take care of a baby sooner than he'd anticipated. If Susan's child was his, these were skills he was going to need. And Jackson really did seem like a good baby. "I'll be okay."

"Are you sure?"

"Positive," Dallas said with more confidence than he felt.

"I'm just in the next room showering if you need me," she said, and he shot her a warning look about mentioning the shower again.

The last thing he needed while he was caring for a baby was the image of her naked in his mind.

His nerves were already on edge and even seeing the baby sleeping so peacefully in his Pack 'n Play didn't help settle them.

"Just go before you put any more images in my mind I can't erase," Dallas said to Kate.

One corner of her lip turned up in a smile and it was sexy as hell.

Watching a sleeping baby had to be the easiest gig ever, he told himself. And yet he could feel his own heartbeat pounding at the base of his throat. His mouth was dry, too. He hadn't felt this awkward and out of place since he'd asked Miranda Sabot to be his girl-friend in seventh grade.

Jackson half smiled in his sleep and it nearly melted Dallas's heart. There was a whole lot of cuteness going on in that baby basket.

There was a knock at the door. Thankfully, the disturbance didn't wake the baby.

Dallas welcomed the delivery from Sawyer Miles, one of the security team members who worked for Gideon Fisher. He thanked him and brought the box into the kitchen.

The pj's were folded on top, so he took those and placed them on the bed in the guest room. Next, he put the food containers in the fridge for later. Dallas returned to the living room and eased onto the chair next to the little boy.

All Jackson had to do was fist his little hand or make a sucking noise for Dallas to jump to attention. Was this what parenting was like all the time? He felt like someone had set his nervous system on high alert. It was fine for a few minutes, but this would be exhausting day and night.

He'd seen that same look of panic on Kate's face more than once in the past twelve hours, and for good reason.

Being alone with a baby was scarier than coming face-to-face with a rabid dog in a dark alley.

Jackson made a noise and Dallas jumped to his feet. He stared down at the Pack 'n Play with more intensity than if there was a bomb ready to explode inside.

The little guy must be dreaming, because he was

making faces. Cute faces. And they spread warmth all through Dallas, which caught him completely off guard. He didn't expect to feel so much for a baby that probably wasn't even his.

The door to the guest room opened and Dallas heard Kate padding down the hall.

He swallowed his emotions.

"Going outside to get some fresh air. Jackson's fine," he said, before she entered the room.

Dallas moved to the back door and walked outside.

The past half hour had been nerve-racking, to say the least. A whole host of emotions Dallas wasn't ready to acknowledge had flooded him. If he was a father, would he be awful at it?

He told himself that knowing Kate was in the shower had him on edge. But it was more than that and he knew it. Being on the ranch had always centered him, no matter how crazy the world around him became. Not this time. His life had spun out of control fast. And he felt nothing but restless.

Distancing himself from Kate and the baby would provide much-needed perspective, he told himself as he tried to regain footing on that slippery slope.

The truth was he liked having Kate and Jackson in his home, way more than he'd expected or should allow. And that caught him off guard. He chalked the sentiment up to facing the first holiday season without his parents.

Then there was the issue of what had happened to Susan and her baby. Dallas hoped both were doing fine. He hadn't thought about babies much before being told that he might be a father. He'd been too focused on making a name for himself, striking out on his own. Not that his last name was a curse, by any means; Dallas had never thought of "O'Brien" as anything but a blessing.

But being a man, he'd needed to make his own mark on the world. Having come from a close family with a man like Pop at the helm had made Dallas want to do his father and himself proud.

Instead, he'd let him down in the worst possible way.

Dallas had always known he'd eventually come back to the land he loved so much and step into his legacy. That was all supposed to happen far off in the future, however.

His parents weren't supposed to die. And it sure as hell wasn't supposed to be his fault.

If they'd only listened to him when he'd said he could arrange to have the unsold art pieces taken back to the art gallery in the morning, instead of insisting on returning them that evening. Then Pop wouldn't have had that heart attack while driving, and both would still be alive.

He couldn't help but wonder if his father would think of him as a disappointment now. Sure, Dallas had been successful in business, but his personal life had always been more important to Pop. Dallas had failed his parents. And he couldn't help but think he'd failed Susan in some way, too.

Not knowing what had happened to her and her baby gnawed at him.

Then there was the news about Morton's death. So much was going on, and Dallas decided that half the reason his attraction to Kate was so strong was that, on a primal level, he needed comfort, proof life could still be good.

He tapped his boot on the paved patio as he gripped the railing. Even the evening chill couldn't snap him out of the dark mood he was in.

He could blame his missteps on working too much, or on his emotional state, but the truth of the matter was he should've known better.

Now Susan might be dead, and he couldn't ignore the weight of that thought or how awful it made him feel.

If he'd told her they could get married, would she be okay?

Maybe he should've strung her along until the baby was born, and all he'd have had to do was swipe a pacifier and send it to the lab for DNA testing. Susan would have never had to know and wouldn't have been in such a desperate state.

Then he'd know for certain if the child was his. He could've arranged help for Susan, and not just with the baby. She needed counseling or something to help get her mind straight.

Dallas stabbed his fingers in his hair as the wind blew a chill right through him.

So many mistakes. So many questions. So many lives hanging in the balance.

He caught a glimpse of one of his brothers out of the corner of his eye.

"Hey," Tyler said. A shotgun rested on his forearm as he approached.

"What are you doing out here?" Dallas asked, before he hugged him.

"We're taking voluntary shifts, walking sections of the property," Tyler replied. "Haven't seen anything suspicious so far."

"Thank you for everything," Dallas said.

"What are you doing out here all by yourself?" Tyler asked.

"Thinking."

"You figure anything out yet?" he said with a half smile. He always knew when to make a joke to lighten the tension.

"Pie is better in my mouth than on paper," Dallas quipped.

"A math joke." Tyler chuckled. "I like it." His expression became solemn. "Seriously, is there something on your mind you want to talk about?"

"Nah. I got this under control," Dallas said. He did want to talk, but surprisingly, not with one of his brothers. He wanted to talk to Kate.

"You always did carry the weight of the world on your shoulders, big brother," Tyler said. "We're here to help if you want to spread some of that around."

"And you know how much I appreciate it," Dallas answered.

They stood in comfortable silence for a little while longer, neither feeling the need to fill the air between them.

"It's going to be different this year," Tyler finally

said with a sigh. He didn't need to elaborate for Dallas to know he was talking about the upcoming holidays.

"Yeah."

"Won't be the same without her holiday goose and all the trimmings at Christmas supper," Tyler murmured.

"Nope." None of the boys had accused Dallas of being responsible for their parents' deaths and none would. He held on to that guilt all on his own.

"You heard anything from Tommy lately about possible involvement from another vehicle?" Tyler asked.

"Nothing new." Dallas rubbed his chin and looked toward the setting sun.

"I get angry thinking about it," his brother admitted.

Dallas nodded and patted him on the shoulder. "Heard Uncle Ezra has been talking to the rest of the family about letting him take over the gala," he said at last.

"You know him—always blowing smoke," Tyler said. "He couldn't handle it alone anyway, and I don't know why he wants his hand in everything."

"Have you spoken to Aunt Bea lately?"

"Heard it through the grapevine that Uncle Ezra has been trying to get her to sell her interests in the ranch to him," Tyler said. "And he's been cozying up with the McCabes, which I don't like one bit."

"Neither do I. That family has been nothing but trouble over the years, and just because Pop is gone doesn't mean I'd betray his memory by bringing them anywhere near the ranch, let alone the gala." Dallas swung his right leg up and placed his foot on the wooden rail off the decking, then rested his elbow on his knee.

"Isn't that the truth," Tyler said. "Uncle Ezra needs to check his loyalty. He wouldn't have anything without Pop's goodwill."

"Unfortunately, not everyone is as grateful as Aunt Bea," Dallas said. "Plus, together they only own five percent of the company. What does he hope to gain by forcing her out?"

Tyler shrugged. "He's making a move for something. We'd better keep an eye on him. Harmless as he seems, we don't know what he's really up to, and I just don't trust him. I don't think Mom ever did, either."

"Good point. She was adept at covering up in front of Pop, but I saw it, too."

The back door opened as the sun disappeared on the horizon.

"Everything okay out here?" Kate asked.

"I better get back to the main house," Tyler said to Dallas.

"Check in if anything changes," he replied, then introduced his brother to Kate.

"Evening, ma'am." Tyler tipped his gray Stetson before disappearing the way he'd come.

"I didn't mean to make your brother feel like he had to leave," Kate said.

"You didn't," Dallas assured her.

"I made coffee in case you want more," she told him, stepping onto the patio and shivering.

"It's cold out here. We can talk without freezing inside." Dallas glanced around, aware that there could be eyes watching them from anywhere in the trees.

This time of year, the sun went down before six o'clock.

"Where's Jackson?" he asked.

"Sleeping in the other room." As Kate walked past him, Dallas could smell the wild cherry blossom shampoo Janis kept stocked, and it reminded him of a warm, sunny Texas afternoon. There wasn't much better than that. "It's been a long day and I'm glad he doesn't realize what's going on."

She'd showered and had changed into the pajamas that had been brought over for her. They'd been pulled from a stash of extra supplies in case guests forgot something at home.

"Good. You found them." The all-white cotton pajama pants and simple matching V-neck button-down shirt fitted her as if they were hand-tailored, highlighting her soft curves.

Dallas forced himself to look away after he caught himself watching a bead of water roll down her neck and disappear into her shirt.

Coffee.

He poured a cup, black, and then paused.

"Think you can sleep?" he asked.

"Probably not," she said with a sigh.

"Coffee sound good? Because I can have some tea they serve at the main house delivered if you'd prefer," he said.

"Coffee's fine. Maybe just half a cup."

YOUR PARTICIPATION IS REQUESTED!

Dear Reader,

Since you are a lover of our books – we would like to get to know you!

Inside you will find a short Reader's Survey. Sharing your answers with us will help our editorial staff understand who you are and what activities you enjoy.

To thank you for your participation, we would like to send you 2 books and 2 gifts – **ABSOLUTELY FREE!**

Enjoy your gifts with our appreciation,

Pam Powers

**SEE INSIDE
FOR READER'S
SURVEY**

For Your Reading Pleasure...

We'll send you 2 books and 2 gifts
ABSOLUTELY FREE
just for completing our Reader's Survey!

YOURS FREE!

We'll send you two fabulous surprise gifts absolutely FREE, just for trying our books!

Visit us at:
www.ReaderService.com

YOUR READER'S SURVEY
"THANK YOU" FREE GIFTS INCLUDE:
- ▶ 2 FREE books
- ▶ 2 lovely surprise gifts

PLEASE FILL IN THE CIRCLES COMPLETELY TO RESPOND

1) What type of fiction books do you enjoy reading? (Check all that apply)
- ○ Suspense/Thrillers ○ Action/Adventure ○ Modern-day Romances
- ○ Historical Romance ○ Humor ○ Paranormal Romance

2) What attracted you most to the last fiction book you purchased on impulse?
- ○ The Title ○ The Cover ○ The Author ○ The Story

3) What is usually the greatest influencer when you <u>plan</u> to buy a book?
- ○ Advertising ○ Referral ○ Book Review

4) How often do you access the internet?
- ○ Daily ○ Weekly ○ Monthly ○ Rarely or never.

5) How many NEW paperback fiction novels have you purchased in the past 3 months?
- ○ 0 - 2 ○ 3 - 6 ○ 7 or more

YES! I have completed the Reader's Survey. Please send me the 2 FREE books and 2 FREE gifts (gifts are worth about $10) for which I qualify. I understand that I am under no obligation to purchase any books, as explained on the back of this card.

❑ I prefer the regular-print edition
182 HDL GKEW/382 HDL GKEW

❑ I prefer the larger-print edition
199 HDL GKEW/399 HDL GKEW

FIRST NAME   LAST NAME

ADDRESS

APT.#   CITY

STATE/PROV.   ZIP/POSTAL CODE

Printed in the U.S.A.
© 2016 ENTERPRISES LIMITED
® and ™ are trademarks owned and used by the trademark owner and/or its licensee.

I-816-SFF15

◀ If offer card is missing write to: Reader Service, P.O. Box 1867, Buffalo, NY 14240-1867 or visit www.ReaderService.com ◀

BUSINESS REPLY MAIL
FIRST-CLASS MAIL   PERMIT NO. 717   BUFFALO, NY

POSTAGE WILL BE PAID BY ADDRESSEE

READER SERVICE
PO BOX 1867
BUFFALO NY 14240-9952

NO POSTAGE
NECESSARY
IF MAILED
IN THE
UNITED STATES

"Cream's in the fridge." He pulled out a jar of sugar and set it on the counter.

She thanked him.

"Can I ask you a question?" Kate perched on the countertop and took a sip of her coffee.

He nodded.

"What's your actual connection to Safe Haven?" Her eyes studied him.

"I already told you that I was investigating them." Not a total lie, but not the truth, either. Dallas drummed his fingers on the counter. "I was in a relationship with someone."

"Susan." Kate's gaze didn't falter. "And you had a baby?"

"There's where everything gets dicey." He paused long enough to see the confusion on her face. "She had a baby. Said it was mine. I'm not so sure."

"You didn't get along with her?" Kate asked, with more of that shock in her voice.

"It's more complicated than that, but the answer would be no."

"What happened?" Those blue eyes stared at him and he wanted to be honest with her.

"I thought she was seeing someone else, and it would have been next to impossible for me to have fathered a child with her," he said. This was awkward, but not as strange as talking to Tommy or the thought of opening up about this to one of his brothers. Why was that? Dallas had known Tommy since they were three years old. And he and his brothers couldn't be closer.

Being the oldest, Dallas had always felt a certain responsibility for taking care of the others. Was he afraid he'd somehow be letting them down by admitting his mistakes?

"Why did she go to Safe Haven?" Kate asked.

"That's a good question. I don't have the answer to it. I had others, so I hired a PI to investigate," Dallas said.

"Wayne Morton," she said.

"That's right. He started digging around. Told me that she'd had a baby and there's a tie to Safe Haven, but I have no idea if the baby was put up for adoption or not."

"I can't even imagine," Kate said, and there was agony in her voice. "That must be the worst feeling in the world."

"Hell can't possibly be worse," he admitted. "Even though I know there's barely a chance I could have a son out there, I can't sleep at night."

"It was a boy?" Kate said, glancing at Jackson's blanket on the couch. "Do you have any idea how old the baby would be now?"

"Maybe three months old," Dallas said, eyeing her reaction.

She glanced at the blanket again and then her gaze fixed on him with a look of sheer panic.

Yeah, he'd noticed the slight resemblance between him and Jackson, but that didn't mean... Did it?

That look of determination came back as Kate squared her shoulders and took a sip of coffee.

"He's not mine," Dallas said, trying to convince

both of them. "All we have to do is swab us both if you want proof."

"I don't need it. Jackson is my son until someone proves otherwise," she said defensively. She hopped off the counter and then walked to the sliding glass door.

It was dark outside, so she wouldn't be able to see a thing. "Don't do that, Kate," he said.

"What?"

"Close up like that." He should know that was what she was doing. He was the king of shutting people out.

She whirled around and there was fire in her glare. "Is that why you've been so nice to us? Because you think Jackson is your son?"

"Hell, no," Dallas said, closing the distance between them in a couple of strides. "And for the record, I *don't* think he's mine. I have more questions than answers, and to say my relationship with Susan was brief puts it lightly."

Kate was too stubborn or too daring to look away, even with him standing toe to toe with her.

And Dallas noticed the second her anger turned to awareness. He could see her pulse beating at the base of her throat, her uneven breathing.

If she planned to walk away, then she needed to do it soon, because he'd made an enormous mistake in getting so close. Close enough that her scent filled his senses and he couldn't think straight anymore.

Before he could overanalyze it, he dipped his head and kissed her.

Her flat palms moved down his chest until her

hands stopped at his waist. She gripped the hem of his T-shirt and he helped her pull it up, over his head and onto the floor.

Dallas spread his feet in an athletic stance, preparing himself to call on all his strength and tell her that this would be a very bad idea. One look in those hungry blue eyes and he faltered.

That was all it took? *Seriously, O'Brien? Way to be strong.*

He brought his lips down on hers with bruising need and delved his tongue inside.

She tasted like a mix of the peppermint toothpaste he kept in the guest room and coffee.

Dallas stopped long enough to close the blinds behind them.

Kate wound her arms around his neck and he caught her legs as she wrapped them around his midsection, their bodies perfectly flush, and then he carried her to the kitchen island.

There wasn't a whole lot of cloth between them as he positioned her on the granite, and he could feel her heartbeat against his bare chest.

Need overtook logic when her fingers dug into his shoulders, pressing him against her full breasts.

Dallas took one in his palm and his erection strained when she arched her back.

He groaned, which came out more like a growl, and felt himself surrender to the moment. He'd never felt so out of control and yet so in the right place in his life. Sex with Kate was going to blow his mind.

An annoying little voice asked if this was a good

idea under the circumstances. And he'd be damned if that unwelcome little voice didn't make a second round, louder this time.

Nothing inside him wanted to stop this runaway train, so he needed Kate to.

He pulled back enough to press his forehead to hers and force his hands on the countertop beside her thighs.

"Tell me this is a good idea," he said, and his breathing was ragged.

Her fingers trailed down his back, stopping at the waistband of his jeans.

"I want it, too," she said, breathless. "But it's a terrible idea."

He sucked in a breath and made a halfhearted attempt to step back.

Sure, he could back off if he wanted to, but the problem was he didn't. He wanted to nestle himself between those silky thighs of hers, free his straining erection and bury himself inside her.

Dallas trailed his finger along the collar of her cotton shirt and down the V. So far, he was the only one with any clothes off. That was about to change. He undid the first pair of buttons on her nightshirt.

Her chest moved up and down rapidly, matching the pace of his own breathing, as he reached up and freed her right shoulder.

Dallas bent low enough to brush a kiss there and then one on her collarbone.

Kate was perfection.

"You're beautiful," he whispered, drawing his lips

across the base of her neck, pausing long enough to kiss her there, too.

She made a move to touch him, but he caught her hands in his. He kissed the fingertips of both before placing them on either side of her.

"No. I get to touch you first."

Her breath caught.

He slicked his tongue in a line down to her breast and gently captured her nipple between his teeth.

"Dallas," she started, her body rigid with tension.

He stopped long enough to catch her eye. "You can tell me to stop at any time and I will. It won't be easy but I won't force this."

"Oh, no. I want you to move faster."

"I can't do that, either," he said. "I move too fast and this will be over before it gets good. And I'm a hell of a lot better than that in bed."

He ran his tongue across her nipple one more time before taking her fully into his mouth, his own body humming with need.

KATE DIDN'T GIVE up control to anyone. Ever. Except for reasons she couldn't explain, she felt completely safe with Dallas O'Brien.

His hot breath on her skin sent shivers up and down her body and caused desire to engulf her. Maybe that was what she needed to clear her head…a night of hot sex with a handsome cowboy.

In some strange way, it felt like she'd known Dallas for more than just a day. But she didn't. He was practically a stranger.

That thought put the brakes on.

She froze and he reacted immediately by pulling back.

"I want to do this, believe me, but I can't." She buttoned the top buttons of her shirt, still trying to convince herself that stopping was a good idea. She had never felt such a strong pull toward someone she didn't know or allowed a situation to get out of control so fast. "I'm sorry."

Chapter Nine

"Tommy just called," Dallas said to Kate as he walked into the living room, thoughts of last night and their almost tryst still a little too fresh in his mind. He figured their emotions were heightened from one seriously crazy day and that was half the reason their hormones got the best of them.

"What did he say?" She was on the couch feeding her son a bottle.

Dallas knew she didn't get a whole lot of sleep last night because Jackson had cried at 10:00 p.m. and then again this morning at three. It was just before eight and he was eating again. Three feedings in ten hours?

For someone who didn't sleep a lot, Kate looked damn good.

"He was able to reach your lawyer," Dallas said.

"What did Seaver say?"

"He made an appointment to drop by Tommy's office today at noon." Dallas crossed the room into the open-concept kitchen.

"I'd like to be there to hear what he has to say."

Dallas nodded. "You want a cup of coffee?"

"That sounds like heaven right now," she said, trying to suppress a yawn. "I usually don't sleep this late."

"This is late for you?" Dallas asked from the kitchen, where he'd started making a fresh pot. Eight in the morning was late for him, too. Work on the ranch began at five in the morning. He hadn't wanted to make noise, so he'd spent the morning recapping the prior day's events.

"I've always been a morning person," she said. "And since Jackson has me up anyway, I'm usually the first one at the soup kitchen. That reminds me. I need to check in at work. I'm sure yesterday has everyone on edge and I still feel horrible about what happened to Allen."

Dallas poured two mugs and brought one to Kate. "You need to keep an eye on his relationship with you."

She thanked him and immediately took a sip. Based on her expression, she wasn't ready to have that conversation.

"Do you really want to work with someone who is fixated on you?" Dallas continued. Knowing he should leave the topic alone didn't stop him from pressing the issue. He was man enough to admit to himself that he was jealous.

"Honestly, work is the last thing on my mind right now," she said, and she sounded defeated.

"You want me to finish that?" he asked, gesturing to Jackson and his bottle.

A moment of hesitation was followed by "No, thanks."

Did she still think he believed Jackson might be his son?

"Last night, about him..." Dallas said. "Well, I just want to reiterate that the probability he's mine is low. I'm offering to help right now so you can have a cup of coffee, not so I can see if there's some parental-child bond between us. Truth is, I'm more than a little uneasy at the thought of holding something that tiny."

The tension in her shoulders relaxed a little as she smiled. "I thought about it all night and maybe we should have a DNA test done today. If your—" she glanced at him "—Susan's child was adopted out through Safe Haven, then we can't ignore the possibility that Jackson *could* be yours."

"It's not impossible but that would be a huge coincidence." Dallas took a sip, enjoying the burn on his throat and the strong taste on his tongue. He thought about the way Kate's kisses had tasted last night. She was temptation he didn't need to focus on.

"Questions are bound to come up and we'll have the answer ready this way."

True. She put up a good argument.

"Chances are strong that I don't have a child at all," he said. "I'm almost certain that Susan was close to someone else at the time we were going out. He may have been the real reason she'd relocated to New Mexico and not to be close to me."

"You didn't confront her about it?" Kate asked.

"Honestly, no. I probably should have but I figured she could see whoever she wanted, given that we weren't exclusive."

"Your girlfriend seeing another man while the two of you were dating was okay with you?" Kate balked.

Dallas couldn't help but chuckle at her reaction. "We weren't serious at the time," he said. "She wanted more and I couldn't give it, at least not then. I thought we could take it slow. Apparently, she had other ideas."

"You didn't break it off?"

"I did," he said. "And then she called a few months later saying she was pregnant and that we should get married."

"Wow. That seems awfully presumptuous. If she was seeing another man, there was no way you could've known for sure the baby was yours." Kate set the empty bottle down and then placed the baby over her shoulder in a fluid motion. She might not have been a mother for long, but she seemed to have the hang of it.

"I'm not making excuses, but when I asked to slow things down until we could get a paternity test, she disappeared," he said.

"Sounds suspicious if you ask me," Kate muttered, bouncing Jackson gently.

"Either way, I need to know." Even if Susan had lied, she sure didn't deserve to be killed, and he hoped that wasn't the case.

"Did you know the guy?" Kate asked.

"No. Didn't want to."

"I can understand that. What about her friends? Think they might know?"

"We don't run in the same circles." She was onto something. If Susan's friends knew who else she'd been dating then they might be able to give them a name, except that his PI had been killed digging around. Maybe he shouldn't involve anyone else.

The baby hiccuped and then burped.

"He's a hearty eater." Dallas changed the subject, eyeing the little boy.

"That's what his doctor says." Kate beamed.

Motherhood looked good on her.

"I called the hospital this morning to check on Stacy, by the way," Dallas said. "She had to have surgery on her shoulder yesterday to remove the bullet. All went well and the doctor is expecting a full recovery."

"That's great news," Kate exclaimed. "And such a relief."

"I had flowers sent over and I thought we could stop by and check on her later."

"I'd like that very much." Kate held Jackson in her arms, looking like she never wanted to let go of him.

Dallas filed that away. There was no way they could bring the baby with them today. It was too dangerous. When he really thought about it, it was too dangerous for Kate, too. She'd been adamant about going yesterday, but after that close call she might change her mind. If Dallas had anything to say about it then she'd stay right where she was. But knowing her, she wouldn't dream of being left out.

"Maybe we could make a detour on the way to the sheriff's office," he said.

"Great."

"Hungry?" Dallas asked.

"Breakfast would be nice."

"I'm not much of a cook, so I had one of my brothers bring over some of Janis's homemade muffins this morning," he said, setting his mug on the side table and moving toward the kitchen.

"Is that what smells so amazing?" she asked, propping Jackson up on a pillow next to her.

Dallas brought in the basket filled with blueberry and banana nut muffins.

"Janis makes them fresh every morning."

"She could run her own bakery, based on the smell alone," Kate said between bites.

"Don't tell her that or we might lose her," Dallas teased.

"Must be hard to find good help," Kate said with a smile.

"My brothers and I kicked in and gave her a share of the ranch. She's worked just as hard as the rest of us in making the place a success." They had figured that she deserved a cut far more than their aunt and uncle, who hadn't put in an honest day's work in their lives.

"That was really nice of you guys." Kate looked impressed.

"It was the right thing to do."

Unfamiliar ringtones sounded, breaking the morning quiet. Dallas quickly realized they were coming from her diaper bag.

She looked around, panicked, and Dallas realized she was trying to figure out how to get to her phone across the room without leaving Jackson alone on a pillow.

"You want me to get that for you?" Dallas asked.

"Would you mind?"

He retrieved her cell and handed it to her. The ringtones were pulsing loudly, but he felt more than their vibration shoot through him when their fingers grazed.

"It's my brother." She looked up at Dallas. "What should I do?"

"Answer it."

KATE TOOK A deep breath and answered.

"What's going on with you?" Carter was frantic. "I've been trying to call and you haven't been answering. A deputy showed up at my house and at Mom's, asking questions."

"We had an incident yesterday morning, but the baby and I are fine."

"Why didn't you call me immediately?" he asked, and she hated the worry in his voice. She still felt like she'd let him down by leaving the business they'd created, and this didn't help.

"I'm sorry, Carter. Yesterday was a whirlwind and I was exhausted." It was partially true. That wasn't the reason she hadn't called, but she didn't want to say that the sheriff had asked her not to.

"Mom is a wreck," Carter said.

"You talked to her?"

"What choice did I have when a deputy knocked on both of our doors? You could've given me a heads-up, Kate." Carter still sounded concerned, but there was something else in his voice she couldn't quite put her finger on. Anger? Frustration? Hurt?

"What did they say?"

"No one told us a thing. They just started asking all these questions about you and Jackson," he said.

What could she tell him? The last thing she wanted to do was lie to her brother.

"Is Mom okay?" she asked.

"After popping a pill and having a glass of chardonnay, yeah. This came as a shock. I mean, you'd think if something happened to you that you'd be the one to let us know," Carter said, and there was a snide quality to his tone.

Was he upset? Concerned?

Maybe that was what was bugging Kate. He seemed more distraught that he and their mother had been surprised than worried about her or Jackson being hurt.

"We were shaken up yesterday, but we're fine now. Thanks for asking," she retorted.

"I figured you were okay, since you answered the phone," Carter snapped.

"What has you so upset? If you're worried about Jackson, he's fine, too," she stated. She didn't like where this was headed one bit.

Had she overestimated her brother's love for her? At the moment, he seemed more concerned with being surprised by a deputy. Then there were his overprotective feelings for their mother.

That stung.

It had always been she and Carter against the world during their childhood and they'd been thick as thieves.

Then again, maybe he resented her more than she realized for leaving the business. She'd sold her shares to him and he'd seemed to be on board with her plan once he got used to the idea.

The times they'd talked, he seemed to be handling

work stress fine. He had a lot on his plate, though, and she figured some of that was her fault.

"Everything okay, Carter?" she asked when he didn't respond, that same old guilt creeping in. Normally, it was reserved for conversations with her mother.

"Sorry, Kate. Mother is just freaking out and I haven't slept in days. We have a new program going live next month at work and I found a hiccup in the code," he said. Now he was beginning to sound like the old Carter. "I've been working twenty-four/seven for a solid week."

Once again she felt bad for leaving him holding the bag even though she'd prepped him far in advance. Still, she knew the stresses of running a business better than most, and of the two of them, she was better at dealing with it.

While she didn't miss the day-to-day operations or the stress, she did miss seeing her brother. Now that they didn't work together and she'd been busy with Jackson, she and Carter had practically become strangers.

"How is the little rug rat who stole you from me?" he finally asked.

"Growing bigger every day."

"Is he allowing you to get any sleep yet?"

"It's better. They don't stay little forever," she said, ignoring Dallas's raised eyebrow.

Their relationship probably did seem odd to an outsider.

"Tell him to hurry up and get big enough to work at the business so his uncle can finally get some sleep," Carter said.

"Sorry. He already said he's going to be a fireman and has no plans to spend his life at a keyboard." Kate could only imagine how this conversation sounded to Dallas, coming from such a close-knit family. *Odd* would most likely be an understatement.

"Mom will be fine," Carter said. "You know her. Breaking a nail is cause for a red alert."

Sadly, that wasn't too much of an exaggeration.

"Have you been spending more time with her lately?" Kate asked, hoping to ease some of her own guilt.

"Not really. Work has been holding me hostage. She'd like to see you, though." Was he trying to make her feel worse about her non-relationship with their mom? Since when was he taking up Mother's cause? "In fact, I better head to the office."

"Oh, where are you now?" Kate asked.

"Nothing. Nowhere. Just out and about," Carter said, and she picked up on the same tone he'd used when he was trying to hide the last candy bar from her when they were kids.

Maybe Mother and Carter were becoming closer now that she was at odds with Kate.

Kate decided not to press the issue, but it ate at her anyway. She should be glad her mom had someone to talk to, since she and Kate's dad hardly ever spoke about anything important. So why did it gnaw at Kate that her mother and brother were on good terms?

Other than the fact that protecting Carter had been half the reason she and her mother had been at odds most of Kate's life?

This suddenly close relationship felt a little like betrayal. Because when Carter had wanted to quit the soccer team at twelve, it had been Kate who'd fought that battle for him, taking on both their parents.

It had been unthinkable for them that Carter wouldn't want to play sports at all. In fact, he'd pretty much hated anything that required him to compete physically. He'd never been the tall, masculine child with a solid throwing arm his father had hoped for and had tried to make him be. Carter had topped out at five foot nine, which pretty much ruled out basketball, a sport their dad had played.

Carter had been great at math, so their parents decided he should be a doctor. That idea fell apart when he couldn't stop vomiting in his high school anatomy class.

It had been Kate who'd stood up to them time and time again on his behalf. She'd let him talk her into the start-up, had worked crazy hours and had sacrificed any kind of social life. Not that she regretted it one bit. She and her brother had been able to do something together that hopefully would last for many years.

"I better go," she said to him now.

"Be careful," he said.

She ended the call, deciding she hadn't had nearly enough rest lately, because she was reading too much into the phone conversation with her brother.

"I've been thinking that maybe you should stay here with Jackson today," Dallas said.

He'd been watching her reactions on the phone and she figured he'd have questions about her family.

"Believe me when I say that I seriously considered

it. In fact, that's just about all I've been thinking about for the past few hours," she said.

"It's risky for you to leave the ranch. And there's no way we can take Jackson with us," he added.

"Both good points," she agreed. Those had been her top two after tossing and turning for a few hours last night.

Jackson started fussing. She picked up her son and cradled him in her arms.

"It would be nice if I had more of his toys here," she said, wishing this whole nightmare was over. "You can't imagine how helpful it is to be able to set him down once in a while."

"I'd be happy to hold him," Dallas offered, and there was just a hint of insecurity in his voice. "On the off chance that I am a father, I probably need to start getting my arms around taking care of a baby, because I have no clue what to do with them."

Actually, he was making a lot of sense.

"It's best if you try this for the first time while sitting down." She stood and walked over to him.

He held out his arms and she placed Jackson in them.

Wow, did that kick-start her pulse.

There was something about seeing such a strong man be gentle with such a tiny baby that hit her square in the chest like a burst of stray voltage. She hadn't thought much about Jackson missing out on having a father before. It struck her now.

Maybe it was the lack of sleep or the thought that

it might actually be nice to have a partner around to help raise her son.

Ever since that little angel had come into her life, she questioned pretty much all her decisions. It would be nice to be able to talk her ideas through or just bounce them off someone else for a change.

Why did all that suddenly flood her thoughts now? She and Jackson had been doing just fine before. Hadn't they?

Wishing for something that wasn't going to happen was about as productive as sucking on a rose petal when she was thirsty.

It didn't change a thing and she'd end up with thorns on her face.

"I hear what you were saying about me sticking around the ranch for safety's sake today. I'd like to be there when the sheriff questions Seaver and I want to visit Stacy in the hospital. It might be nice for her to have another woman around. I didn't get the impression she had anyone to talk to," Kate said.

"Same here," Dallas said.

"Plus, I feel guilty that those men showed up at her office to begin with. I'm worried that my car drew them to her," she said.

"When they didn't find Jackson with us, they disappeared." Dallas looked down at the baby. He was beginning to look more at ease.

Her son being in the cowboy's arms filled her with warmth.

"I'll need to figure out something to do with him

while we're gone," she said, chalking her emotions up to missing her brother.

"Janis offered her assistance when I asked for baby supplies," Dallas said. "She doesn't know who's here, but I'm sure she suspects it's you, since she met you yesterday."

"She's one of the few people I would actually trust with my son," Kate said, and she meant it. Plus, there was the fact that she was already at the ranch and the security here was top-notch. Dallas had given Kate the rundown. There were armed guards at all three entrances and cameras covering most other areas, especially near the houses.

Although the entire acreage couldn't realistically be completely monitored, and there were plenty of blind spots, no one would get anywhere near the houses without being detected.

That thought would've let her sleep peacefully if the handsome cowboy hadn't been in the bed right down the hall.

Chapter Ten

"I meant what I said earlier." Dallas shifted the baby fidgeting in his arms. Was the child just as uncomfortable as him? Was that why the little guy was squirming?

Sure, holding Jackson felt good in a lot of ways. But he was so little that Dallas was afraid he'd break him without realizing it. Could he break a baby?

This felt like middle school all over again, when he'd had to carry that egg around for a week. Dallas had broken his on the first day. And he'd already seen how many broken bones his brothers had endured while playing with him.

Jackson started winding up to cry and Dallas's shoulders tightened to steel. "I'm afraid I'm not very good at this." He motioned toward the baby with his head. He was afraid to move anything from the neck down.

And it didn't help that Kate was cracking a smile as she walked toward them.

"You think this is funny?"

"It's just a relief to know I'm not the only one who was nervous when I held him those first few times. I thought it would feel so natural to hold a baby, but it didn't." She reached his side, but instead of offering to take her son, she perched on the arm of the leather chair.

"I'm glad my pain bolsters your self-image," Dallas quipped, feeling even more tense as the first whimpers came.

"Sorry. It just reminds me how hard it actually was for me in those early days and how far I've come since then." She placed her hand on his shoulder. "I'm convinced babies can read our emotions. The more we relax, the more they do."

Relaxed wasn't the first word that would come to mind if Dallas was trying to describe himself.

Jackson wound up and then released a wail. Dallas felt a little better knowing that Kate's presence had done little to calm the child.

"And then sometimes he just needs a good cry," she said, finally taking him from Dallas.

As she did, he got a whiff of something awful smelling. She must have, as well, because her nose wrinkled in the cutest way.

"I think someone needs a diaper change," she said as she moved Jackson to the couch and placed him on his back.

"You need help with that?" Dallas asked.

She waved him off and went to work.

"Have you ever done this before?" she asked.

"Nope." He was mildly curious and figured he'd need to know all about it at some point when he became a father.

"Me, either. Well, not until Jackson." She finished taping the sides of the fresh diaper and then tucked his little legs inside his footed pajamas. "I put the first one on backward and didn't realize it until he had a leak. I'd also bought a size too big."

"Sounds complicated."

"You get the hang of it," she reassured Dallas, neatly folding the used diaper. "We may not want to keep this inside the house."

He held out his hand.

"You sure about that?" she asked.

"I'll have to get used to it at some point in my life, right?"

She nodded.

When he returned from taking it to the garbage out back, she was pacing. "When should we go?"

"Anytime you're ready, if you're certain you want to leave the property."

"Part of me wants to stay right here and never leave," she said, pensive. "I feel safe here and I don't want to let go of that feeling. But whoever is trying to take Jackson away from me is still out there and I need to do everything I can to find him or my son will never be safe."

Dallas understood that logic. He could see all her emotions in her determined blue eyes.

And he tried not to focus on the other things he saw there...

DALLAS'S BOOTS CLICKED against the tiled floors of the hospital wing. The nurse had said Stacy was doing fine when he'd called to check on her last night. He needed to see for himself.

There was a secondary reason for his visit. Maybe there was additional information he could get out of her. Yesterday had felt like a waste of time and he wanted to do everything he could to help locate Morton's killer. Adding to Dallas's guilt was the feeling that he'd put Stacy in harm's way by showing up at her office with Kate.

Stacy was sitting up when he and Kate reached the opened door.

"Come in," she said. Her eyes were puffy from crying and she had a wad of tissues balled in her right fist. Her hair was piled high on her head and she wore a blue hospital gown.

The room was standard, two beds with a cloth curtain in between. It was opened, since the second bed was empty. Stacy's was closest to the window.

"How are you feeling today?" Kate asked, making it to her side in a beat. She had a way with people that made even the worst situation feel like everything would work out all right.

He chalked it up to motherhood. Kate had the mothering gene. Not everyone did. He couldn't imagine that Susan would have that same effect on people. She had good qualities, but was more the invite-to-happy-hour personality than the soothing type.

Of course, being close to Kate brought up all kinds of other feelings Dallas didn't want to think about. And the sexual chemistry between them was off the charts.

He mentally shook off the thought, focusing on Stacy instead.

"Thank you so much for the beautiful flowers." She motioned toward the bouquet on the side table.

Dallas nodded and smiled.

"Did they catch those guys?" she asked.

"Afraid not," he said. Tommy had promised to call or text the moment they were in custody, and so far, Dallas hadn't heard anything. Whoever was behind this had sophisticated ways to disappear when they needed to and that set off all kinds of warning bells for Dallas.

It had also occurred to him that Susan could've gotten herself into some kind of serious trouble. Now that his investigator was dead, there was no one chasing her trail aside from Tommy. And the problem with that was the fact that his friend wouldn't be able to share a whole lot of information about a murder investigation in progress.

So Dallas needed to come up with a plan of his own without stepping on the sheriff's toes.

"Did you get a look at the men?" Dallas asked. He'd been able to give a basic description to law enforcement of dark hair and medium build, before Stacy had blocked his view, which didn't rule out a lot of people in Bluff.

"No, it was a blur," she said. "Everything happened so fast. All I remember seeing was the end of a gun and then a blast of fire, followed by a burning sensation in my shoulder. Once I put two and two together, I honestly thought I was going to die."

Dallas could see why she'd focus on the barrel, given that the gun was fired at her a moment later. "I want to catch these bastards but I need your help," he told her.

"What can I do?" Her gaze bounced from him to Kate and back.

"I'd asked about secret files before. I know you'd never want to betray Wayne's trust, but I need to see mine and any others he has."

"If he had files like that, I didn't know about them." She glanced down, which usually meant a person was lying or covering.

"What about his laptop?" Dallas asked.

"It was in his car," Stacy said, which meant Tommy or one of his deputies was already tearing it apart.

Dallas paced, trying to think of another way to come at this, because he was fairly certain Stacy was holding back. Since his straightforward approach was bringing up an empty net, he needed to take another tack.

"It's okay if you don't know," Kate assured her. "He just wants to find the guy who did this to Wayne."

Stacy glanced at Kate and the softer approach seemed to be baiting her. "Isn't the sheriff already working on it?" she asked.

"Yes, he is. And we would never do anything to get in the way of that. But these guys are dangerous and they might come back for you if they think you know something," Kate said calmly. "And I think we can help with the investigation."

Stacy stared at the door.

Dallas turned to look out the window, because whatever Kate was doing seemed to be working.

"They have his laptop from the office," Stacy finally started, "but that's not where he would keep a secret file, because it would be the first place people would look if he was subpoenaed."

"He's smarter than that, isn't he," Dallas said, turning toward her.

Stacy half smiled and a deep sadness settled in her hazel eyes. "Yes. He was."

Dallas gave her a minute to recover. "I lost someone very important to me a few months ago," he finally said. "Actually, two people."

"I remember reading about your parents in the newspaper and thinking it was a tragic accident," Stacy said wistfully. "I'm real sorry about that, because I'd always heard they were fine folks. Real down-to-earth types. It must've been hard to lose both of your parents like that and especially…"

She glanced up at him with an apologetic look on her face but couldn't seem to finish her sentence without breaking down.

"Thank you," he said. "I know what it's like to have people taken away before their time. And, yes, the upcoming holidays make it worse. Believe me, very soon, once the initial shock wears off, you're going to be angry."

Stacy nodded, blowing her nose into a wadded-up tissue.

"You already want answers and so do we," Dallas said. She was getting close to trusting him; he could tell by the change in her demeanor. "You already know that I could have a child, a son. And I need to know if

Wayne found something that got him in trouble while working on my case."

Shock registered on her face, but to her credit she recovered quickly.

"Family has always been important to an O'Brien, and I'm no different. Losing my parents makes me value it even more," he said. "I have selfish reasons for wanting to get that file. Wayne was most likely killed because of my case…because of something he found. If I know what that is, I have a chance at finding out if I have a son and nailing Wayne's killer. Plus, the whereabouts of my son's mother is unknown. She might be in trouble. You and I both know the sheriff may never figure it out since he has to work within the law. And even if he does, it might be too late."

Dallas believed Tommy could dissect pretty much anything given enough time. But that was one luxury they didn't have. As sheriff, he would have to go through proper channels and file paperwork that could take days, weeks or months to process.

"I hired Wayne," Dallas said. "His death is on me. And I need to find out what he knew."

A tear rolled down Kate's cheek. She quickly wiped it away.

Stacy was already blowing her nose again. "He spoke very highly of you," she said. "I didn't know at the time that it was *you*. He referred to your case as Baby Brian. Now I realize it was because of O'Brien."

"Help me find the jerks who did this to him, who shot him in cold blood," Dallas said. "You have my word you'll be the first to know when I do."

Stacy sat there for a long moment, her gaze fixed out the window.

"Will you hand me my purse? It's in the bottom drawer over there," she finally said, motioning toward the nightstand near the bed. "The deputy brought it to me last night when he stopped by."

Kate retrieved the Coach handbag and Dallas noted the designer brand.

Stacy glanced up at Kate and then Dallas as she reached for it. "This was a gift from Wayne." She finally dropped the pretense that the two of them had had a strictly professional relationship.

Kate reached over and hugged her, and the woman sagged onto her shoulder.

"He was all I had," Stacy said. "I never really had a family. He took a chance when he hired me five years ago, because I was nothing. I didn't know a laptop from a desktop. He said he could send me to training for that. Loyalty was the most important thing to him. I could do that. Our relationship was a professional one for the first three years and then, boom, something happened."

"You fell in love," Kate whispered.

"It was like a lightning bolt struck one day and there was no going back," she agreed. "We kept things a secret because Wayne was afraid of someone using me against him."

Kate touched her hand and Stacy looked up with glassy, tearful eyes.

"I'm sure he wanted to do whatever was necessary

in order to protect you. He must've loved you very much," Kate said with calm reassurance.

More tears flowed, and even though Dallas was in a hurry to get information, he didn't want to rush out of the room. He was glad that he and Kate could be there for Stacy, and especially since she'd lost her entire support system in one blow.

"I don't know what I'm going to do now," she said. "I don't have a job or a purpose. Wayne showed me his will last year. He left everything to me, but what do I do when I leave here without him?"

There was a lost quality to her voice that seared right through Dallas.

"If you ever want to work again, there'll be a job waiting for you at the ranch," he said. "Once you get your bearings."

"You would hire me without knowing anything about me?" Stacy looked almost dumbfounded.

"Wayne was a good man. I trust his judgment," Dallas said. "Call my cell whenever you're ready and let me know what you decide."

He pulled out a business card and dropped it on the nightstand.

"And the soup kitchen always needs good people," Kate offered.

"That means a lot," she said. "I'm not sure what I'll do at this point, but this gives me options."

Loyalty was important to Dallas, too. And Wayne was right. An employee could be trained for pretty much everything else.

Stacy rummaged around in her purse until a set of

keys jingled. She pulled them out and held them on her left palm. With her right hand, she picked through them until she stopped on one.

"This is the key to our house," she said, locking eyes with Dallas. "I'll write down the address for you."

He nodded before she returned her attention to the keys and thumbed through a few more.

"I kept all the keys on one ring, but I also made a duplicate just in case." She pulled out a piece of paper and pen, and then she scribbled the address.

"This little baby right here opens his office door at home," she stated. "There's a house alarm. I'll give you the code. And another one for his office."

Dallas would expect nothing less from an investigator of Morton's caliber.

Next, she dumped the contents of her purse onto the bed. She had a matching wallet, a pair of Ray-Ban sunglasses, a pack of gum and sundry items like safety pins and paper clips.

As she turned the bag inside out, Dallas saw a glint of something shiny inside. Metal? A zipper?

"This purse was made special," she said, unzipping it.

She shook the bag and a key fell out.

Chapter Eleven

"This one unlocks a compartment in a book called *Save for Retirement*. It's on the bookshelf behind his desk in his office, on the second shelf. It should be the second volume from the right. It works like a diary," Stacy said, motioning toward the key. "There'll be a flash drive inside. I never looked at it, wasn't supposed to, so I didn't. I can't tell you what's on that drive for certain. But whatever he found out about your case, I'd bet my life it would be there."

She held out the keys toward Dallas.

"Thank you," he said as he took them.

Kate hugged Stacy again and he could plainly see that she didn't want to leave the woman alone.

"Mind if I send someone over to keep an eye on you while you rest?" Dallas asked. "I don't like you being here without protection."

"Guess I didn't think about it, but you're right. I'd appreciate that very much," Stacy said.

Dallas made a quick call to Gideon Fisher to put the wheels in motion and then settled in to wait for backup to arrive. Fisher said he'd send Reece Wilcox.

Stacy was on medication, and even though she seemed wide-awake and alert, he didn't want to risk her falling asleep and being vulnerable until Reece arrived.

Kate retrieved the remote and put on one of those home decorating shows to provide a distraction for Stacy. Mindless TV was the best medicine sometimes.

"Can I get you anything from downstairs?" Kate asked. "Or order out?"

"No, thanks. I'm fine. The food here isn't horrible." Stacy paused long enough to wipe at a tear. "You can't know how much I appreciate you both."

For the next twenty minutes, they all sat and watched a kitchen makeover in comfortable silence.

By the time Reece showed up, Dallas and Kate were due at the sheriff's office.

They said their goodbyes to Stacy and promised to visit again as soon as they could.

In the parking lot, Kate put her hand on Dallas's arm.

He stopped and turned to face her, but before he could speak, she pushed up on her tiptoes, wrapped her arms around his neck and kissed him. Hard.

KATE HAD MEANT to brush a quick "thank you" kiss on Dallas's lips, but her body took over instead and she planted one on him.

His arms looped around her and dropped to her waist, pressing her to his muscled chest.

Dallas O'Brien was the very definition of *hot*. But he was also intelligent, kind and compassionate. Traits she didn't normally associate with a rich cowboy. He also had a down-to-earth quality that was refreshing. Her body seemed to take notice of all Dallas's good qualities because heat flooded through her even though it couldn't be much more than thirty degrees outside.

When he deepened the kiss, she surrendered.

Instead of fighting her feelings, she tightened her arms around his neck and braided her fingers together. The motion pressed her breasts against his chest even more and her nipples beaded inside her lacy bra.

Neither made a move to break apart when he pulled back a little and locked his gaze with hers.

They stood there, only vaguely aware that it was frigid outside, because inside their little circle was enough warmth to heat a room, and Kate's heart filled with it.

She'd never known this kind of appreciation and acceptance from anyone.

Certainly not from her mother or father. During her childhood, when the two spent time with her, it had felt sometimes as if they were ticking off boxes on a duty list rather than spending real time with her. And then there was her failed marriage to Robert. He'd been handsome and they'd been attracted to one another, but she'd never felt…this, whatever *this* was. More than anything, he just seemed ready to take the next step when the time came. Had their relationship, too, been a box he'd needed to tick off at that point in his life?

Gazing into Dallas's dark, glowing eyes, she saw something she'd never seen when looking into another man's. Rather than analyze it, she kissed him again, because Dallas O'Brien stirred up emotions she didn't even know how to begin to deal with.

And she lost herself in that kiss.

Dallas pulled back enough to whisper in her ear, "You're beautiful, Kate."

She loved the sound of her name on his lips. "So are you."

He laughed at being called beautiful. But he was, inside and out.

His phone dinged, and he checked the screen and then showed it to her.

William Seaver had just checked in at the sheriff's office.

"This is to be continued later," Dallas said, taking her hand in his, lacing their fingers together. He led her to his truck, which had been retrieved by a member of security last night, his gaze sweeping the area as they walked.

Ten minutes later, he parked in the lot at the sheriff's office.

"I hope we didn't miss anything," she said.

"If I know Tommy, he'll hold off the interview until we get inside." Dallas surveyed the lot before ushering her into the office, a reminder of how dangerous their situation still was.

Tommy greeted them in the hall before leading them to his office. "I spoke to Mrs. Hanover last night."

"What did Susan's mother say?" Dallas asked.

"That the last time she heard from her daughter was three months ago," Tommy said.

"What did she remember about their conversation?"

Dallas perked up. He seemed very interested in what Tommy had to say and who could blame him?

"She told her mother that she was going out of the country for a while and not to worry about her," he said. "Told her she'd get back in touch when she could."

"That makes me think she planned to disappear," Dallas said. "She knew that she was in trouble."

"That's my guess," Tommy stated.

"This is the first positive sign we have so far that Susan could still be alive," Dallas said.

"Would she just give up her baby and take off?" Kate asked. Those actions were inconceivable to someone like her, but Dallas didn't seem surprised.

"If her child really had been mine, it seems out of character that she'd give up so easily on proving it to me," Dallas said after a thoughtful pause.

"She would've had the paternity test done, the results made into a necklace, and then worn them on a chain around her neck," Tommy stated.

Dallas nodded. "Gives me a lot to think about."

"Sure does," Tommy said. "Let's see what Kate's lawyer has to say."

Tommy urged them into his office. Then he brought in the attorney.

"You already know Kate Williams," Tommy began, "and this is Dallas O'Brien."

Seaver barely acknowledged Kate. What was up with that?

He looked guilty about something, but Kate couldn't pinpoint the exact reason.

Her lawyer's eyes widened when he heard the O'Brien name, a common reaction she'd noticed and figured was due to the status of Dallas's family. Even she'd heard the name before she moved to Bluff, albeit briefly, and that was saying something.

"You represented Miss Williams in her adoption from the Safe Haven Adoption Agency, correct?" Tommy asked.

"Yes, I did." Seaver's eyebrows arched. "Why am I being asked about that? Miss Williams is right there and she can tell you everything."

"We appreciate your patience with the question," Tommy said, redirecting the conversation. Seaver was midfifties and wore a suit. His round stomach and ruddy cheeks didn't exactly create the picture of health.

"Did you know that Miss Williams's home was broken into yesterday?" Tommy pressed.

Seaver seemed genuinely shocked. "Why would I know that?" he asked, crossing his right leg over his left. "I don't live around here, Sheriff. Have you looked at anyone locally?"

"Whoever did this walked straight to her desk. Isn't that strange?" Tommy continued.

"I guess so. Maybe they were looking to steal her identity," Seaver guessed but he seemed tense.

"People usually search the trash for that information," Tommy said.

"What does any of this have to do with me?" Seaver asked.

"Nothing, I hope," Tommy quipped. "But on that

file, the stolen one, was her adoption records. Now, why would anyone want those?"

"Good question. And one that I don't have an answer to," Seaver said, but his eyes told a different story.

It struck Kate as odd because he was practiced at presenting his side of an argument and maintaining a blank face, having done so a million times in court. And yet he seemed unnerved.

"A man tried to abduct Miss Williams's son yesterday, as well. Guess you don't know anything about that, either," Tommy murmured.

Pure shock and concern crossed Seaver's features. His top button was undone and his tie was loose around his neck. He leaned forward. "Look, I never dealt with the guy, but this sounds like the work of Harold Matthews. I've heard rumors about him setting up adoptions and then staging abductions. He works for Safe Haven and that's the reason I specifically requested Don Radcliffe. I don't know if any of the rumors are true, mind you. But that's where I'd look first."

"Could Radcliffe and Matthews be working together?" Tommy asked.

Seaver took a second to mull it over. "It can't be ruled out. I've placed a dozen babies through Radcliffe and this is the first time anything like this has happened."

Tommy asked a few more routine-sounding questions before asking for the list of clients with whom he'd placed babies from Safe Haven.

"I can't do that without a court order," Seaver said, tiny beads of sweat forming at his hairline.

"I'm asking for your cooperation, Mr. Seaver," Tommy countered.

"Look, I don't mean any disrespect, but I'm not about to expose clients who have requested and paid for private adoptions to anyone, not without a signed order from a judge," he said, folding his arms and then leaning back in his chair. "And especially not for a failed abduction attempt and a break-in."

"Then you must not have read today's paper," Tommy said.

Seaver blew out a frustrated breath. "Where is this going, Sheriff?"

"A man was murdered yesterday in connection with investigating Safe Haven Adoption Agency," Tommy said matter-of-factly.

A startled look crossed Seaver's features before he quickly regained his casual demeanor. "I've already told you everything I know. But for my money, I'd locate Harold Matthews." The lawyer pushed himself to his feet. "And if there are no more questions, I have other appointments to attend to today."

"I'll be in touch," Tommy said, also standing.

"I have no doubt you will, but you want to talk to Matthews, not me," he said as he walked out the door.

"I think he's lying," Dallas said when he'd left.

"What makes you say that?" Kate asked.

Before Dallas could answer, Tommy called Abigail into the room. "See if we can get a subpoena for William Seaver's client list as it relates to Safe Haven," he said.

"The judge has been downright cranky lately," she said. "I'll do my best to convince him."

Tommy thanked her. "Another thing before you go. I need everything you can get me on Harold Matthews. Search Don Radcliffe, too. If either one of those men have had so much as a parking ticket in the past year, I want to know about it."

"Will do," she said, before padding out the door and then disappearing down the hall.

"There's another way to go about this," Tommy said, turning to Dallas. "We need to step up our efforts on connecting the existing kidnappings to Seaver. It might take some time. If there's a link, we'll find it. Don't leave until I get back."

"I have a new theory," Dallas said, stopping his friend at the door. "What if Seaver is the kidnapper? He was a little too quick to pass the blame and give names. And he sure as hell seemed nervous to me."

Tommy leaned against the jamb, folding his arms. "I noticed that, as well."

"Has he been to the soup kitchen?" Dallas asked Kate.

"Yes. That's where we met right after the adoption," she said, still stunned at the thought.

"Was Allen around?" Dallas asked and she immediately knew what he was thinking. Seaver might've set up Allen as cover. But why would the lawyer try to take Jackson?

"As a matter of fact, yes," she responded. "But how would he know about Allen's feelings for me?"

"It's obvious to everyone," Dallas said quickly, and there was a hint of something in his voice. Jealousy? "Seaver knew you and could have easily arranged to set up Allen with the pictures," he added.

"I'm still missing motive," Tommy said.

"He might not be the one pulling the strings," Dallas said.

Tommy was already rocking his head. "If whoever was behind the kidnappings thinks Seaver arranged an adoption they didn't want to happen, then they could be pressuring him to find the infant."

"Exactly what I was thinking," Dallas said.

"Which would confirm our earlier thoughts that someone wants their son back and they're willing to do whatever it takes to find him," Kate said. An icy chill ran up her arms.

Deputy Lopez's voice boomed from the hallway.

Tommy ushered him inside his office.

"Three more of the adoptions shared the same lawyer," Lopez said.

"Let me guess… Seaver?" the sheriff asked.

Lopez nodded. "But here's something you don't know. Two of the babies were found today…"

Kate cringed, waiting to hear the next part as she prayed for good news.

"Both alive," Lopez said.

"Where?" Tommy demanded, before anyone else could.

"One was left at a baby furniture store two towns

over, in one of the cribs for sale. An employee discovered the sleeping infant an hour after she opened, and called local police, who were able to make the match," the deputy stated.

"And what about the other one?" Tommy asked.

"He was left at a church, discovered before service began. Pastor said he'd been in the chapel half an hour before and there was no baby."

"Neither boy was hurt?" Tommy asked, with what could only be described as a relieved sigh.

"Not a hair on their bald heads," Lopez quipped with a smile.

"How long were they missing?" Tommy asked.

"A few days."

"Enough time for a proper DNA test," he mused.

This was good news for everyone except Kate. Some kidnapper was trying to find his own son and checking DNA of all the possibilities before giving them back. And that was fantastic for all the mothers of those babies, because it meant they were in the clear. Jackson, however, was still in question. There was a scrap of hope to hold on to, since the babies were being found alive. Extreme care was being taken to ensure that the infant boys were being located quickly.

Except what if Jackson was the one they were searching for...?

Kate closed her eyes, refusing to accept the possibility.

Tommy excused himself and the deputy followed.

"Seaver lied about not knowing the other family whose baby was abducted," Kate said.

Dallas nodded. "I picked up on that, too."

"What do we do now?" she asked. Dallas hadn't told his friend about the keys from Stacy and Kate hadn't expected him to, given that they'd received them in confidence.

"We have to wait for dark for our next move," he stated, with a look that said he knew exactly what she was asking.

Which meant they'd spend at least another whole day together.

"It's only a few weeks until Halloween. You have a party to help plan. I don't want to get in the way of your family," she said. All she had in the house was a three-foot fake ghost that said "Happy Halloween" and then giggled every time it detected movement. She'd nicknamed him Ghost Buddy and he was all she'd had time to put out. Even though she knew Jackson wouldn't remember his first Halloween, she wanted to find a way to make it special. Ghost Buddy was her first real decoration and she figured that she could build her collection from there.

The thought of going home scared her because the more they dug into this case, the less she liked what they found and the more afraid she felt.

The only bright spot was that a couple more of the babies had turned up and they were fine.

Tommy returned a moment later. "I agree with you, by the way. I think Seaver's lying."

"Which means he's either involved or covering for someone who is," Dallas said.

"He gave us a name," Kate offered.

"That might have been meant to throw us off the real trail, buy some time or take himself off the suspect list," the sheriff said.

"Or dodge suspicion," Dallas added. "He seemed awfully uncomfortable."

"I noticed. I wanted to keep him here but he knew better than anyone that I had nothing to hold him on." Tommy nodded. "At least we have a few leads to chase down now. In the meantime, I think it's safer for the two of you on the ranch."

"You have my word that we won't leave unless we have to," Dallas said. "What did you learn when you interviewed Stacy last night?"

"Not much," Tommy said with a sigh. "She didn't recognize the guys and couldn't give much of a description other than what the gun looked like."

"Sorry that we couldn't help with that, either," Dallas said. "Unfortunately, my back was turned for the few seconds we were in the room, and Stacy blocked my only view of their faces, brief as it was."

"She's going to be okay," Kate interjected. "She's strong."

"I sent over security," Dallas said. "Wasn't sure if the guys would come back and I didn't want to take any chances, just in case someone got worried she could testify against them."

Tommy thanked him. "I'll let you know if we get the subpoena or any hits on linked cases," he added.

"What can you tell me about the murder scene yesterday?" Dallas asked.

"Nothing stood out. It will take time to process the site, but it looks like a standard forced-off-the-road-and-then-shot scenario."

Kate winced. How could any of that be run-of-the-mill?

And then it dawned on her why the voice at Stacy's office sounded familiar. "It was him. The other day at Morton's office. The guy who tried to take Jackson."

Dallas's head was rocking. "I couldn't put my finger on what was bugging me before. That's it."

Tommy added the notation to the file.

Dallas's phone vibrated. He checked the screen and the brief flicker of panic on his face sent her pulse racing.

He muttered a few "uh-huh"s before saying they were on their way and clicking off.

She was already to her feet before he could make a move. "What's going on?" she asked.

"There was a disturbance on the east side of the property. A motorcycle tried to run through the gate," he said, quickly reassuring her that no one got through and everyone was just fine.

She wished that reassurance calmed her fast-beating heart. It didn't.

"You want me to send a deputy?" Tommy called, as they broke into a run.

"I could use an escort," Dallas shouted back.

Kate's chest squeezed and she couldn't breathe.

No way could she allow those men to get near her son.

Chapter Twelve

Dallas raced through the city with a law-enforcement escort clearing the path. He'd enter the property on the west side near his place, because there was more security at that checkpoint. The earlier ruckus had been on the opposite side, miles away, and if he was lucky, he and Kate would be able to slip in from the west before anyone else could realize what he'd done.

Things were escalating and the kidnappers seemed to be zeroing in.

The thought did occur to Dallas that the attempted breach could be a distraction meant to get him and Kate out in the open. Or someone inside, if he took another vantage point. The latter wouldn't succeed, because there was plenty of security at all the weak spots on the ranch. If the former was the case, then it was working, and he had to consider the possibility that he was playing right into their opponents' hands.

Still, he had to take the chance. One look at Kate and he knew she needed to hold her baby in her arms after the disturbing news about Seaver.

He had her pull out his cell and call his head of security. "Put the call on speaker," he instructed.

She did and he could hear the line ringing almost immediately.

"We're close, about five minutes out," Dallas said to Gideon Fisher, his security chief, when he answered.

"I'll be at the gate and ready, sir," Fisher responded. "Ryder and Austin are here, with a team of my men."

"Excellent." Dallas knew all the extra security at the gate would alert anyone watching to the possibility they'd be coming in that way, but his brothers knew how to handle a rifle and Dallas wanted the extra firepower in case anything went down. "Where's everyone else?"

"Tyler's up front. Colin's roaming."

It sounded like his brothers were ready to go, in addition to the staff of eight…well, seven, since Reece stood vigil in Stacy's hospital room.

A sport-utility vehicle with blacked-out windows roared up from behind.

Dallas's truck was sandwiched between the deputy in front and the SUV barreling toward their bumper.

"Hold on," Dallas told Kate, just as the SUV rammed into them, causing their heads to jolt forward.

"Sir?" Gideon said.

"We have company and we just took a hit," Dallas replied.

"Roger that, sir."

Dallas could see the entrance to the ranch in the distance. Once inside, they'd be safe, but it was dicey whether or not they could get there.

He flashed the high beams to alert their escort to the trouble brewing behind him. The deputy must've noticed because he turned on his flashing lights. "Black SUV, stop your vehicle," the officer called out over his loudspeaker.

The SUV rammed them once more, again throwing their heads forward.

"Change of plans." Dallas gunned the engine and popped over into the other lane of the narrow country road. He was lucky that there was so little traffic in the area and this stretch of road was straight and flat, so there'd be no surprises.

The deputy slowed to allow Dallas safe passage, but the SUV whipped into the left lane, as well, maintaining close proximity to Dallas's bumper.

Even repeating the message over the bullhorn didn't work. The other driver persisted.

Dallas got a good look at him in the rearview and he wore similar clothes to the kidnapper at the soup kitchen. He'd bet money it was the same person.

Worse yet, when Dallas moved into the right lane again the SUV pulled up beside him, blocking his turn.

Austin stepped onto the road and aimed his rifle directly at the oncoming vehicle. Dallas pointed and the driver must've noticed, because he hit the brakes. Before the deputy could respond, the SUV had made a U-turn and was speeding off in the opposite direction.

The deputy followed in pursuit, lights flashing.

Dallas turned onto his property, and that was when he

finally glanced at Kate, whose face had gone bleached-sheet white.

She didn't speak and he didn't force the issue.

As soon as he parked in front of his house, she practically flew out of the truck. "Is Jackson in there?"

"Yes." Dallas followed her inside as she ran to her infant son.

Janis met her in the living room, a sleeping Jackson in her arms, and immediately handed him over. She seemed to know that Kate wouldn't care if the baby woke. She had to hold him.

The look on Kate's face, the same damn expression from yesterday morning, cut a hole in Dallas's heart.

Jackson wound up to cry, then belted out a good one. The boy had strong lungs.

Kate cradled her son while Janis excused herself.

The crying abated a few minutes later as Kate soothed her baby, and the sight of the two of them together like that stirred something in Dallas's heart.

He didn't want to have feelings for anyone right now.

The timing was completely off, now that he was chasing down what had happened to Susan. Besides, he was busier than ever, between the ranch and the business. He was helping Kate and didn't need to confuse his feelings for more than that.

Dallas excused himself to work in his home office.

He hadn't turned on his computer in a few days and that would mean an out-of-control inbox. He'd seen the emails rolling in on his smartphone, but he'd been too busy to give them much thought.

Then there was the ranch to run, and Halloween Bash just around the corner.

After answering emails until his eyes blurred, he stretched out his sore limbs while seated in his office chair.

The stress of the past few days was catching up with him and at some point he'd need to sleep. There wasn't much chance of that as long as Kate was in the house. His mind kept wandering to her silky body curled up on the bed in the guest room, her soft skin…

Just thinking about it started stirring places that didn't need to be riled up. Especially since there was no chance for release.

So he focused on his inbox again, wishing he'd receive an email or text from Tommy stating that they got the guys in the SUV.

The next time he glanced at the clock, it was three o'clock in the afternoon. The house was quiet. He'd worked through lunch, which wasn't unusual for him. His stomach decided it was time to eat.

Work might have distracted him for a little while, but more and more he wondered what had happened to Susan. Given Morton's death and both their associations with Safe Haven, Dallas feared the worst.

There were 437 messages in his spam folder and he checked each one to see if Susan had tried to contact him but her note had gotten hung up in his filter.

Nothing.

He pulled the set of keys Stacy had given him from

his pocket, set them on his desk and lazily ran his fingers along them.

Granted, he and Susan had no business being a couple, but he still felt angry at the possibility of something bad happening to her.

Was she in trouble when she'd called him and told him about the baby? Had she been hoping for his protection? He'd assumed all along that she was trying to trap him into marriage, and she had been, but now that he'd seen the look on Kate's face when it came to a threat to her son, another reality set in. Susan might have been desperate and looking for protection. Marriage to Dallas might've been a way for her to secure her son's future.

She had to know that Dallas would've figured out the truth at some point if the child hadn't been his. Then again, if her life had been in danger, she might have figured she'd tell him after the deal was sealed.

Saying he was the father could've been the equivalent of a Hail Mary pass in football, a last-ditch effort to save the game.

Frustration nipped at his heels like a determined predator. Dallas searched his memory for anything he could remember about the last conversation they'd had before she'd gone missing, and he came up empty.

His cell phone buzzed. The call was from Tommy, so Dallas immediately answered.

"I have news," his friend said.

"What did you learn?"

"We got a few hits today. Of the six abductions

that we know about so far, four of them used Seaver," Tommy related.

"So most likely he was involved in the others," Dallas reasoned.

"True. And there's something else."

"Okay," Dallas said.

"Don Radcliffe was found dead in his apartment in Houston."

"Isn't that who Seaver worked with at Safe Haven?" Dallas asked.

"It was."

"Any word on Harold Matthews?"

"We can't locate him. But he's roughly the size and shape of the man you described as the kidnapper from yesterday morning," Tommy replied, then paused for a beat. "Are you alone?"

"Yeah. Why?"

"I have personal news." The ominous tone in his friend's voice sat heavy in Dallas's thoughts.

"What is it?" he asked.

"At first I thought I should wait until all this is over, but I figured you'd want to know the minute I found out. It's about your parents. I got a report from the coroner a couple of days ago that indicated your mother had a heart attack," Tommy said quietly.

"What are the chances of both my parents having a heart attack on the same day?" Dallas asked.

"It made me suspicious, too, so I requested a lab workup. The toxicology report came back showing cyanide in both of their systems. Enough to cause heart attacks," Tommy said.

"What does that mean, exactly?" Dallas was too stunned to form a coherent thought beyond that question.

"I'm opening a formal investigation into their deaths and I wanted you to be the first to know."

Those words were like a punch to Dallas's gut.

"I know it's a lot to process right now, and I may not find anything, because ingestion could've been accidental," Tommy added. "But I'm not leaving any stone unturned when it comes to your parents."

Dallas sat there. He couldn't even begin to digest the thought that anyone could've harmed his parents.

"Dallas, are you still with me?" his friend asked.

He grunted an affirmation, then drew a deep, rasping breath. "Is it possible that their accident might have been staged?"

"Yes, but I'm not ready to jump to any conclusions just yet."

The line went quiet again. Because the implication sitting between them was murder.

"You know I'm here for you anytime you want to talk," Tommy said at last.

Dallas realized he was gripping his cell phone tight enough to make his fingers hurt. "Any word on the SUV? Because the driver easily could've been the kidnapper from yesterday."

"It disappeared and we lost the trail."

THE NIGHT WAS pitch-black and the temperature had dipped below freezing. The wind howled. At least Jackson was with Janis, in a cozy bed sound asleep.

Kate's teeth chattered even though she wore two layers of clothing underneath her coat.

She and Dallas had decided to wait until after dark to go to Wayne's house, reasoning that if they left too late, then dogs in the neighborhood might give them away. He'd parked four blocks over.

Ever since she woke from her nap, she'd noticed something was different about Dallas. His mood had darkened and he'd closed up.

Was he preparing himself for the news as to whether or not he was a father?

He had to have considered the possibility that if he'd had a son, the boy could've been targeted in the kidnappings, as well.

At nine o'clock, lights were still on and households busy with activity. Dallas put his arm around Kate's waist and even through the thick layers she felt a sizzle of heat on her skin.

Wayne Morton's house was on a quiet lane in a family neighborhood. Smoke billowed from chimneys on the tree-lined street of half-acre lots. The crisp air smelled of smoke from logs crackling in fireplaces. Halloween lights and decorations filled front yards.

There were enough neighbors about that she and Dallas could slip in and out of Morton's house without drawing attention.

As Kate walked down the sidewalk, tucked under Dallas's arm, she could see kids in the front rooms watching TV or reading on couches, their mother's arms curled around them.

Someone whistled and then called out, "Here, Dutch. Come on, boy."

A tear escaped before Kate could sniff it away. She turned her face so Dallas wouldn't see her emotions, while wondering what it must be like to have a mother's unconditional love and acceptance. She wished that for her and Carter.

Another person half a block down was rolling a trash can onto the front sidewalk for weekly garbage pickup.

"Morton's place is on the next street," Dallas said in a low voice, interrupting her thoughts.

When she didn't respond, he glanced at her.

A second, longer look caused him to stop walking. He turned until they were face-to-face.

Another errant tear escaped and he thumbed it away.

"Are you okay?" He spoke and she could see his breath in the cold air.

Instead of speaking, she nodded.

Dallas's thumb trailed across her bottom lip and then her jawline. Kate had never known a light touch could be so sweet, so comforting.

A set of porch lights turned off across the street and they both pulled back.

Dallas laced their fingers together as they strolled down the lane.

As Morton's house came into view, Kate couldn't help but notice it was the only one on the street that was completely blacked out. That image was sobering and a sad feeling settled over her, making walking even more difficult.

Thinking of Stacy in the hospital, how sad she'd been, made Kate feel awful. Would she come home to an empty, dark house in a few days when she recovered? How would she get past this? Wayne, her job, seemed to be her life. She'd said they were all she had. Before Jackson had come into Kate's life, she could relate to feeling empty inside. And now with Dallas in the picture, she'd never been more aware of how alone she'd been when she was married to Robert.

Dallas stopped at the bottom of the stairs, clearly as affected by the scene as Kate was. She could see guilt so clearly written in his expression. There was something else in his eyes when she really looked closer. It dawned on her what: he might be about to find out if he was a father.

Worse yet, if his child had been adopted out to a stranger, then Dallas might never find the little boy. Given the nature of closed adoptions and the privacy of all involved, it would take moving heaven and earth to locate the baby, and Dallas O'Brien didn't strike her as the kind of man who could live with himself if he had a child out there somewhere and didn't know him.

"Are you ready for this?" she asked.

A car turned onto the street two blocks down.

Dallas glanced around. "As ready as I'll ever be."

The layout was just as Stacy had described. Dallas ushered Kate inside, closing and locking the front door behind them as she disarmed the alarm. The office was to the left of the foyer and had double French doors with glass panels.

There was enough light coming from the surrounding houses with the Halloween lights on for them to see large objects like furniture.

Dallas slid the office key into the lock and then paused to take a fortifying breath.

Here went nothing…

Chapter Thirteen

Dallas stepped through the door and quickly found the next keypad, to punch in the code for the office.

They kept the lights off so as not to alert anyone who might be driving by or watching the place that they were there.

Inside the office, Dallas located a few books and brought them to the window. Stacy had said the volume they wanted would be on the second shelf, two books from the right. She hadn't told them there would be a wall of bookcases to choose from.

A beam of light flashed from outside. A cop?

That would so not be good. Kate froze and held her breath until the beam moved across another window.

What the heck was that?

She didn't know and didn't want to ask questions. Fear assaulted her as memories from yesterday invaded her thoughts. The men, the guns…

She took a deep breath to calm her frazzled nerves. Getting worked up wouldn't change a thing. They'd still be in a dead man's house going through his things. And even that didn't matter as much as getting back to Jack-

son safely. Janis had taken him to the main house to
sleep tonight, and Kate's heart ached being away from
him. Even though she wouldn't see him until morning,
being back on the ranch would calm her racing pulse.

She moved to another bookshelf and pulled out a
couple of volumes, making her best guess where the
right one would be. Then she stepped next to Dallas
at the window, where there was more light. One of the
books was definitely less heavy than the others. She'd
noticed the instant she'd slid it from the shelf.

Disappointment filled her when she opened the
lighter book. Nothing.

She and Dallas moved on to other bookcases and
flipped open more volumes, placing them back as
closely as possible to their original spots.

"I think I have it," he said at last, making tracks to
the window to get a better look. He held his offering
up to the light. "Yep. This is it."

A noise from the alley caught their attention. Dallas grabbed her hand and moved toward the door in
double time.

"It's probably just a cat, but we don't want to stick
around and find out," he said.

"What if someone's watching the house?" she asked,
ignoring the sinking feeling in the pit of her stomach.
Adrenaline had kicked in and her flight response was
triggered. She needed to get the heck out of there more
than she needed to breathe.

"Stay calm and pretend like we're supposed to be
here." Dallas checked the peephole before opening
the door. So far, the way looked clear, but he couldn't

be certain no one was out there. He tucked the book under his coat, thinking about the meeting he needed to set up with his brothers in the morning to deliver Tommy's news about their parents.

Right now, he needed to get Kate and himself the hell out of there and back to the ranch.

After locking the door behind them, he led Kate down the few steps to the porch. That was when he heard the telltale click of a shell being engaged in the chamber of a shotgun.

"Where do you think you're going?" a stern male voice said. "Turn around and put your hands where I can see them."

"Don't panic," Dallas whispered. "Do as he says and we'll be fine."

Dallas turned slowly to find himself staring down the barrel of a shotgun. Behind it was a man in his late sixties with white hair and a stout build. Dallas had spent enough time around law-enforcement officers to know that this guy had been on the job. He wore pajama bottoms, slippers and an overcoat.

"What are you doing here?" the man asked.

"We just stopped by to check on the place for a friend," Dallas said, figuring this was more a friendly neighborhood-watch situation than a real threat. He couldn't relax, though. This guy looked like he meant business.

"Does this friend have a name?" the man asked, business end of the shotgun still trained on Dallas.

"Wayne Morton," Dallas replied, hoping that would

be enough. "He and Stacy are out of town and asked us to keep an eye on the house."

"That right?" The guy eyed them up and down suspiciously.

Kate stepped closer to Dallas and put her arm around him. "They're friends of ours and I'd appreciate it if you wouldn't point that thing at us."

The man lowered the barrel, much to Dallas's relief. It was too early to exhale, however.

"You should turn on the porch light," the man said. "And it's dark in the alley. There's a light back there, too."

"Will do," Dallas said, although he'd pretty much agree to anything to walk away from this guy without raising suspicion.

"Honey, we have to go. Babysitter's waiting," Kate said, twining her fingers in his.

"Thanks for the tip," Dallas said with a nod. His chin tucked close to his chest, staving off the cold. He decided keeping it there would shield his face. A man who used to be paid to notice things wasn't a good one to have around.

"When's Morton coming back?" the guy asked.

"In a few days," Dallas said, praying he hadn't read today's newspaper.

That seemed to satisfy the neighbor. Dallas could hear his feet shuffling in the opposite direction. He glanced back just in case and was relieved to confirm the man was heading home.

If this guy was watching the PI's house, then others could be, too. And that got Dallas's boots moving a little faster.

Another sobering reality struck him.

The data on the thumb drive tucked away in the book he held on to could change his life forever.

The weight of that thought pressed heavy on his shoulders as he drove back to the ranch.

"I don't think Stacy should go home until we figure all this out," Kate said, breaking the silence between them as he pulled onto the ranch property.

"Agreed," Dallas said, thankful to focus on something else for a minute. Another thought had occurred to him. The information on that drive might tell him what had happened to Susan. And at least one area of his life could have resolution, even as more questions arose in others.

Whatever was there might be valuable to someone. Morton could be dead because of the information gained since he was on an investigation for Dallas when he was killed.

And then there could be nothing relevant on it, too. Dallas was just guessing at this point, his guilt kicking into high gear again. There were so many emotions pinging through him at what he might find on that zip drive.

Dallas gripped the steering wheel tighter as he navigated his truck into his garage.

"I doubt I'll be able to sleep without Jackson here," Kate said, and he could hear the anguish in her voice.

"You want me to have him brought over from the

main house?" Dallas asked. "I can make a call and he'll be here in ten minutes."

"No. I don't want to wake Janis after she was nice enough to help care for him in the first place." Kate sighed wistfully. "He's probably asleep anyway, and waking him up just so I can look at him seems selfish."

"I can send a text to have her bring him over first thing in the morning, as soon as they wake," Dallas offered, turning off the engine. "In fact, she probably left a message already, letting us know how the night went. I silenced my cell phone before we left."

He fished the device from his front pocket and then checked the screen as he walked in the door to the kitchen. "Yep. Here it is," he said, showing it to Kate.

Her eyes lit up and they felt like a beacon to Dallas. Everything inside him was churning in a storm.

There was a picture of her sleeping baby, with one word underneath: *angel.*

"Thank you," Kate said, tears welling.

"I didn't mean to make you cry." Dallas held the phone out to her. "You can hang on to that if you want. I need to check the contents of this drive."

"Mind if I come with you?" she asked. "Or I can stay out here if you'd like some privacy."

Normally, that was exactly what he would want.

"I'd rather you be with me when I take a look," he said, and he surprised himself by meaning it. As crazy as everything had been in the past few days, and as much as his own life had been turned upside down even more in a matter of minutes, being with Kate was the only thing that made sense to him.

She set his cell phone on the counter, took his hand and once again laced their fingers together. Rockets exploded inside his chest with her touch.

"Ready?" she asked.

"As much as I can be," he said, and the look she shot him said she knew exactly what he was talking about.

They walked into his office hand in hand and Dallas couldn't ignore how right this whole scenario felt. It seemed so natural to have her in his home, which was a dangerous thought, most likely due to an overload of emotions.

Dallas sat in his office chair and Kate perched on one of his knees. He had to wrap his arms around her to turn on his computer, and that felt so good. A big part of him wanted to lose himself in her and block out everything else.

Another side of him needed to see what was on that flash drive.

His computer booted up quickly and he mentally prepared himself for what he would find. There could be nothing at all, and that would bring a disappointment all its own.

Dallas needed answers and yet there was a healthy dose of fear exploding inside him at finding the truth.

He plugged in the device and a few seconds later a file popped up in the center of the screen.

Dallas clicked on the icon with a foreboding feeling. He scanned a couple of documents.

"Okay, from what I can tell so far, Wayne tracked a baby to Safe Haven and that's where the trail ends," Kate said. "Which is what we already knew."

That about summed up what Dallas had seen, as well. And, no, it wasn't helpful.

"Here's the odd thing. Once the baby was born, Morton seems to think Susan disappeared," Dallas noted. He also realized that the dates didn't rule out the possibility that Jackson was his son.

"And, like, seriously vanished," Kate mused. "No more records of her exist anywhere. I mean, I guess I can see that she might have had a closed adoption, and the agency would have coded her file so as not to give her identity away. That happened with mine. The birth mother wanted a sealed adoption and I was in no position to argue. Plus, I thought it would be better anyway. But there should be some trail of her somewhere—an address, credit card, cell-phone record."

"Her bank account has been closed. There's no record of her existence."

"It's almost like she died," Kate said.

"But then, wouldn't there be a record of that?" Dallas shoved aside the thought that Kate's baby could actually be Susan's.

This was not the time for that discussion. First things first, and that meant Dallas needed to figure out if he was a father.

He opened the other documents one by one, scanning each for any link to his and Susan's baby. If there was one.

There was nothing.

Morton had been thorough and yet… Dallas opened the last file. It was labeled WS.

"Morton questioned your attorney the day before he was killed," Dallas said.

Kate's eyes were wide. He could see them clearly in the reflection from the computer screen.

She opened her mouth to speak but no words came.

"We need to have that DNA test. It's the only way we'll know for sure that you're not Jackson's father," she said.

"If that's what you want. I can arrange one in the morning," Dallas told her.

She muttered something under her breath. She'd spoken so low, Dallas wasn't sure he heard right.

Should he be offended?

"I hope you know that I'd make one hell of a fine father someday," he said, a little indignant. His emotions were getting the best of him.

Kate turned those blue eyes on him and his chest clutched.

"I didn't mean to insinuate that you wouldn't be a good father. You would." Her eyes were filled with tears now. "It's just Jackson's all I have. My relationship with my parents is practically nonexistent. My brother and I used to be close and now he's siding with my mother, which stinks, considering how little she supported either one of us growing up."

Dallas's arms tightened around Kate's waist, and that was a bad idea given the mix of emotions stirring inside him. A very bad idea.

Tears streamed down her beautiful face. Dallas wanted to say something to make it better, and yet all he could manage was "I'm sorry."

"No. I don't expect you to understand, and I'm embarrassed to say anything. I have Jackson now and he's my world," she said.

"I can see that he is," Dallas assured her.

"And he's enough. All I ever wanted was to have a family. Is that too much to ask?" She buried her face in her hands and released a sob.

"It's not," Dallas said. "And I understand more than you know. Because I have an amazing family, I know exactly how much we build each other up, rely on each other. I can't imagine where I'd be if I didn't have my brothers by my side, and especially since we lost our parents."

He lifted her chin until her gaze met his, ignoring the rush of electricity coursing through his body. It took heroic effort to turn away from the pulse throbbing at the base of her throat.

"You're an amazing mother," he stated, and she immediately made a move to protest. "Don't do that to yourself. You are. Jackson is lucky to have you and you're doing a great job. Don't doubt that for a second."

"I'm scared," she admitted, and it looked like it took a lot to say those words. Someone as strong as she was wouldn't want to concede to a weakness. Dallas knew all about that, too.

"It's okay," he said reassuringly.

"What if I lose him? What if my adoption turns out to be illegal and someone has a claim on my son? I've read stories like that." She stopped to let out another sob.

"It won't happen."

"That's impossible to say right now," she said. "I could lose him and that would destroy me. He's all I have."

"You might not have had friends when you came to town and you might've been too busy to make any since. But you have me now. And any one of my brothers would stand behind you, as well. Plus you've found a friend in Stacy."

"You're kind to say that, but we've only just met," she said, her gaze searching his to find out if there was any truth to what he was saying.

"We may have known each other for just a few days, but that doesn't mean I don't *know* you," Dallas said calmly. He considered himself a good judge of character and any woman this devoted to her child couldn't be a bad person. She put Jackson first every time. Period.

In some deep and unexplainable part of his heart, he knew Kate.

THERE WAS SOMETHING about Dallas O'Brien's quiet masculinity and deep voice that soothed Kate's frazzled nerves. It shouldn't. She shouldn't allow it. But *shouldn't* walked right out the door with self-control as she leaned forward and kissed him.

The instant her lips touched his, Kate knew she was in serious trouble, and not just because she might be sitting across a courtroom from this man someday fighting for custody of her son. Everything in her body wanted to be with Dallas, and that should stop her.

He deepened the kiss and his hands came up to cup her face.

And there wasn't anything she could do to resist what her body craved. With him so close, his scent filled her senses and her heat pooled between her thighs. It had been a very long time since she'd had good sex and her body craved release that only Dallas could give. Normally, it took time to get to know a man before she'd let her guard down and allow him to get this close. But she'd never been *this* attracted to anyone. With Dallas, it felt right, and her brain argued that there was no reason to stop. From a physical sense, her brain was right: she was an adult; he was an adult. They could do whatever they wanted. Her heart was the holdout.

Except that the logical voice that generally stopped her from making life-changing mistakes was annoyingly quiet.

And she wanted Dallas O'Brien with her entire being.

Her hands tugged at the hem of his gray V-neck shirt. The cotton was smooth in her hands as she pulled it over his head and dropped it onto the floor.

This time, there was no hesitation on either of their parts. No stopping to make sure this was right.

Her shirt joined his a moment later and the growl that ripped from his throat sent heat swirling.

"You're incredible," he said, his hands roaming across her bare stomach.

And then he cupped her breast and it was her turn to moan. His lips closed on hers as though he was swallowing the sound.

His hands on her caused her breasts to swell and her nipples to bead into tiny buds. Her back arched involuntarily and she wanted more…more of his hands on her…more of his touch…more of his clothes off.

Kate stood, unbuttoned her jeans and shimmied out of them, kicking off her shoes in the process. Her bra and panties joined them on the floor.

And then she stood in front of Dallas naked.

His hands came up to rest on her hips and he pressed his forehead against her stomach.

One second was all it took for him to decide. No words were needed.

And then in a flash he was standing and she was helping him out of his jeans and boxers.

He lifted her onto the desk and rolled his thumb skillfully across her slick heat.

"I'm ready." It was all she needed to say before the tip of his erection was there, teasing her.

She clasped her legs around his midsection as he drove himself inside her. She threw her head back and rocked against his erection until he filled her. She stretched around his thick length.

"You're insanely gorgeous," Dallas groaned, pulling halfway out and then driving deep inside her again. She met him stroke for stroke as he stroked her nipple between his thumb and forefinger, rocketing her to the edge.

She grabbed on to his shoulders, her fingers digging into his muscles to gain purchase.

Stride for stride, she matched his pace, until it became dizzying and she was on the brink of ecstasy with no chance of returning.

The explosion shattered her, inside and out, and she

could feel his erection pulsing as he gave in to his own release. He stayed inside her as she collapsed on the desk, bringing him with her, over her.

He brushed kisses up her neck, across her jawline, her chin.

And then he pulled back and locked eyes with her.

"You know one time isn't going to be enough, right?" And the sexy little smile curving his lips released a thousand butterflies in her stomach.

Chapter Fourteen

Dallas woke at five o'clock the next morning, an hour before his alarm was set to go off. Kate's warm, naked body against his in his bed made it next to impossible to force to get up.

The moment he eased from beneath the covers, he regretted it. He walked lightly to his office so he wouldn't disturb her sleep. He needed to make a call to Tommy and fill him in on what they'd found out last night. And there was so much information making the rounds in his head after learning the news about his parents. He was doing his level best not to jump the gun straight to murder when it came to them, knowing he might be grasping at straws to shift the blame away from himself.

He threw on a fresh pair of boxers and jeans and then moved into the kitchen to make coffee.

"Seaver's involved up to his eyeballs," Dallas said to Tommy over the phone, taking his first sip of fresh brew. His friend had always been an early riser, awake and on the job by five.

"Do I want to know how you know this?" his friend

asked, and there was more than a hint of frustration in his voice.

"Morton visited him the day before his death," Dallas insisted, not really wanting to go there with the lawman.

"That's not exactly an answer."

"Just talk to him again. Believe me when I say it'll pay off," Dallas said.

"I'd love to. The problem is I have to walk a fine line with him," Tommy stated. "And it takes time to pull together evidence."

"He killed Morton to silence him. I'm sure he did." Dallas knew full well his words weren't enough to go on. They required proof.

"That may be true, but I need more than your hunch to get a search warrant for his house or his bank accounts," Tommy said. He blew out a frustrated breath.

Dallas knew his friend was upset at the situation and not at him. He shared the sentiment 100 percent.

"I hear what you're saying and I know you have to do this the right way to make it stick, but trust me when I say he knows more than he's telling." Could he share what he'd found on the data drive? He hadn't obtained it illegally, and yet he felt Stacy should be the one to make the call.

"I can put a tail on him. That's about the best I can do under the circumstances." Tommy blew out another frustrated breath.

Speaking of Stacy, did Seaver know about her and Wayne? Dallas wondered.

"I'm probably going to regret this, but what makes you think he shot Wayne Morton?" Tommy asked.

"Believe me when I say it's more than a hunch. Can you check his tire treads to see if they match the ones at the scene?" Dallas asked.

"Already getting someone on it," Tommy said, sounding like his coffee hadn't quite kicked in yet. "Did you get any word on Susan?"

"As a matter of fact, I did." He could share that, since, technically, he'd paid for that information and part of the data belonged to him. "Here's the thing with her. When she disappeared from New Mexico, it's like she vanished. No more paper. One day she was there and then it was like she never existed."

"She get involved with a criminal who made her go away?" Tommy asked, his interest piqued.

"Wouldn't there be a paper trail? Apartment lease? Something?" Dallas asked. "I mean even in the worst-case scenario there'd be a death certificate."

"True." Tommy got quiet. "Not to mention the fact that she was living in New Mexico. Why use a Texas adoption agency?"

"I'm figuring that she was hoping her child would grow up close to home," Dallas said. "I'd have to think there'd be a missing person's report on her somewhere, right? But you checked and there isn't."

"Where'd you get your information?" His friend clicked keys on his computer. "Never mind. Don't tell me. I don't want to know."

"Is there anything you can use to link Seaver to

Morton's murder?" Dallas asked. "Any evidence that might've been overlooked?"

"Tire tracks are iffy, at best. I doubt I could convince a judge to give me what I want based on just that little bit of evidence, so even if they match he'll say so do the tracks of a hundred other vehicles," Tommy muttered. "I'll check to see if Seaver owns a gun. Might get lucky there and get a caliber match from ballistics."

"I've been thinking a lot about Allen Lentz," Dallas said. "About him being set up. Seaver met him, and my instincts say he decided to take advantage of that crush Lentz has on Kate."

"Given his computer skills, Lentz should've been able to cover his tracks better," Tommy agreed. "Maybe I can find a link there."

"We know the kidnapper didn't act alone. If this was a crime of passion, then Allen would've acted on his own, wouldn't he?" Dallas asked, ignoring the knot in his gut as he thought of another man making a pass at Kate.

"That's a safe bet. Allen seemed to think there was still a chance with Kate. If all hope had been lost then he might be motivated to do something more extreme. She seemed to be dodging his advances without outright rejecting him," Tommy said.

"The guy attempting the kidnapping was fairly young. I'm just trying to cover all the bases, but is there any chance Allen could've hired someone?" Dallas asked.

"Nothing from his bank account gives me that impression. No large withdrawals in the past few months."

"What about neighbors?"

"Everyone alibied," Tommy stated.

"Seems like Lentz can be safely ruled out as a suspect," Dallas said.

"That's where I'm at with him," Tommy confirmed. "Good to look at this from all angles, though."

That gave Dallas another thought. "Could someone else be pulling the strings with Seaver?"

"That's a good question," his friend said. "One I hope to answer very soon. So, yes, it's a definite possibility."

Dallas hoped to have an answer, too. Because Kate's future was hanging in the balance.

"I'll do my best to track down Susan using my means," the lawman told him.

"I'd like that very much," Dallas said. "And thank you for looking into my parents' situation. I'll tell the family this morning."

"I'm not making any promises, but if there's something foul, I'll figure it out," Tommy said.

Dallas thanked his friend again, ended the call and then checked the clock. It was almost five thirty. He'd received a text from Janis. She and Jackson were up and she was about to give him his bottle. She said they'd be there around six.

He could wake Kate up for another round of the best sex of his life before the baby showed up. Or he could fix another cup of coffee.

He stood up and turned toward his bedroom.

KATE ON HIS BED, in his bed, had Dallas wanting more than just a night or two with her. But what else? When this was all over, he needed to sort out his emotions and figure out exactly where he saw this relationship fitting into his already overcrowded life.

Relationship? Was that what was happening between them? Something was different, because for the first time in his life, Dallas had no clue what his next move was going to be.

She stirred and they made love slowly this time.

"I'll grab you a cup of coffee," he said, kissing her one last time before leaving the bed.

"Really?" She stretched and the move caused her breasts to thrust forward. The sheet fell to her waist as she sat up, and all he could see was her silky skin. "'Cause I could get used to this."

"Good," he said, thinking the same thing as he forced his gaze away from that hot body and walked toward the hallway.

By the time he fixed her coffee, Kate was dressed and Jackson was coming through the front door in Janis's arms. Dallas couldn't help but notice that the older woman was beaming.

"Thank you for taking care of him," Kate said, reaching for the baby.

He smiled and that was all it took for her to beam, too.

"It was truly my pleasure. I married young, but we never were able to have children," the older woman said wistfully. "Lost my Alvin to the war and never found anyone I could love as much."

She waved her hand in the air and sniffed back a tear. "No need to get sentimental before coffee. I enjoyed every minute spent with this little man and I hope you'll let me watch him again real soon."

Janis cooed at Jackson, who smiled as Dallas grasped two mugs of coffee.

"You staying?" he asked Janis, gesturing with a cup.

She was already waving him off. "No. I better get back to the main house. There's been a lot of excitement lately and it's best if everyone feels like it's still business as usual."

"You sure? I make the best coffee on the ranch," he said persuasively.

She held out a hand and pretended to let it shake. "Already had half a pot. If I drink any more we'll have an earthquake going."

"Keep me posted if anything happens at the main house," Dallas said.

"I have a few appointments scheduled, planning for the Halloween Bash. Should I have them rescheduled, or plan to meet those individuals for lunch in town?" she asked.

"Off property might be best for now," he agreed. "Until we can sort out everything that's happening and be sure everyone's safe."

"I thought you'd say that," she added, as she excused herself and moved to the front door and then looked at Kate again. "He's an awfully gorgeous baby. Don't you think so, Dallas?"

"As far as babies go, this one's all right," he said

with a wink to Kate. He set her coffee mug next to her and looked at mother and child.

Could the three of them, and possibly four, if he was a father, ever be a family?

He'd known Kate Williams for just a few days and was already thinking about a future with her?

That made about as much sense as salting a glass of tea.

Dallas mentally shook off the thought. He'd gone without sleep for two nights and it had him off balance. Plus there were the holidays and the recent news about his parents. He was grateful his ringtone sounded, providing a much-needed distraction.

It was Tommy.

Dallas answered. "I'm putting the call on speaker so Kate can hear."

She looked up from where she sat on the floor playing with Jackson.

"I have news about Susan," his friend said.

"What did you find out?" Dallas moved closer to Kate.

"Your guy was right. She disappeared. As in cleaned out from the system," Tommy revealed.

"What does that mean? A person can't just vanish, can they?" Kate asked, astonished.

"There's only one way I can think of," Dallas said. "Could she have been placed in a witness protection program?"

"It's the only thing that makes sense," Tommy agreed. "I should be able to pull up some record on her, but they just stopped right around the time her baby would have been born. And there's no report of her hospitalization."

"So she knew she'd be going into the program during the pregnancy," Dallas said, realizing that was most likely why she'd wanted to get married. She wanted the baby to have a normal life, and Dallas was the only person capable of protecting her son. Which brought him back to his initial question... Was he the father?

"Seaver's missing. We'll bring him in for more questions as soon as we locate him," Tommy added.

"Wait a minute. I thought you put a tail on him." Dallas took a sip of coffee, needing the jolt of caffeine. If he understood things correctly, finding Susan was a complete dead end. People in the witness protection program didn't randomly show up again. The only way to figure out if he was the father of her child would be a DNA test of the baby, but he had no idea where the little tyke was or whom he was with.

Speaking of Susan, she'd said a few things to him that made Dallas think she must've wanted a normal life for her child, and that was why she'd given him up for adoption. Dallas would bet money that she'd used Harold Matthews at Safe Haven to handle the paperwork for her or handle the adoption without paperwork. Even if Tommy could get a subpoena for Safe Haven's records, which was highly doubtful, that paperwork most likely wouldn't exist. The agency administrators would be smart enough not to keep records for an under-the-table adoption, especially if the Feds were somehow involved.

Seaver must know something about Susan, and that was why he was involved.

Pieces started clicking together in Dallas's mind.

"I have a theory about what might've happened," he said. "Susan was in over her head with someone. This person was involved in illegal activities and she decided to turn state's evidence against him, putting her and her baby's lives in danger. She didn't want that for her son, so she arranged an adoption through Safe Haven."

"Why Safe Haven?" Kate asked. "Why not somewhere far away?"

"She loved this area, grew up here. When she asked me to marry her, she wanted to move back home with the baby. I'm guessing she wanted her son close to her hometown so she could keep an eye on him when she returned at some point later down the road," Dallas theorized.

"Makes sense," Tommy agreed. "She might've given the stipulation to her handler that her son would be allowed to grow up in or near Bluff, Texas. If the guy she was involved with found out about the adoption, he could be targeting babies here."

"To get back at her or draw her out of hiding," Dallas finished. The one bright spot in this crazy scenario would be that Susan was alive and doing well in the program.

"There's another possibility worth considering. The bad guy might be the father, and he found out about the baby," Tommy said. "The recent spate of kidnappings could be him or his henchmen looking for his son. There was a child discovered in his carrier in the baby-food aisle of a Piggly Wiggly last night. A DNA test this morning confirmed he was one of the boys abducted from an adopted family."

"Which means that all the boys who were kidnapped have been returned home safely?" Dallas said, glancing at Kate.

He wasn't quite ready to let himself off the hook with Susan just yet. Sure, she might've been grasping at straws in telling him he was the father, but there was still a slight chance that it was true. He hoped that she was alive, thriving somewhere else, and that her baby was safe. "Until we know for sure, I'm going to stay with the assumption that the boy could be mine."

"I understand your position," Tommy said. "And that's fine to think that way. I'm looking at the facts and I have to disagree."

"What's the next step?" Dallas asked. He appreciated his friend's perspective, hoped he was right.

"Locate Seaver. Get him in for questioning and try to trip him up," Tommy replied. "I already sent someone to pick up Harold Matthews. You mentioned before that you knew Susan was seeing someone else when you two dated. Think you can work with a sketch artist to give me a visual of the guy?"

"Yeah, sure."

"I don't like you leaving the ranch, so I'd rather send someone to you with a deputy escort."

"What time do you think you can have someone sent over?" Dallas asked. He had a few things he needed to take care of in the meantime. Top of the list was calling his brothers together for a family meeting.

"I can probably have someone over by lunch," Tommy said.

"Let me know if you get Seaver in for questioning between now and then. I'd like to be on the other side of the glass when he's in the interview room," Dallas said.

Tommy agreed and they ended the call.

"I'd like to go see myself what Seaver has to say," Kate said, holding Jackson. "I just wish there was something to identify him at the scene of Wayne's murder or connect him in some way."

"So do I. Speaking of which, I want to check on Stacy this morning." Something was gnawing at the back of Dallas's mind.

Kate nodded. "I need to check in at work afterward. Make sure everything's going smoothly at the kitchen. I can't relax, because I have the feeling that I'm dropping the ball somewhere."

"The curse of leading a busy life. It's hard to slow down long enough to notice the roses, let alone stop long enough to smell them," Dallas agreed.

"Do you work all the time when you're not helping strangers?" she asked with a half smile.

Kate was beautiful and her looks had certainly made an impression on Dallas. There was so much more to her. She was kind, genuine and honest to a fault. Intelligent.

There wasn't much she couldn't accomplish if she set her mind to something.

"Do you have any idea how amazing you are?" He kissed her forehead, wishing he could whisk her into the bedroom again. Not an option with the little guy around. Besides, Dallas needed to get his brothers together and then work until the sketch artist arrived.

She rolled her eyes and smiled up at him. "I doubt it."

She'd built a successful company from the ground up. She ran a successful nonprofit while taking care of one of the cutest darn kids Dallas had ever set eyes on.

He had a hard time believing that she could feel inadequate in any way.

If he had to describe her in one word it would be… *remarkable*.

"You're kidding me, right?" he asked.

"Growing up in my childhood home didn't inspire a lot of confidence." She rolled her shoulders in a shrug.

"Then I wish you could see the person I see when I look at you." And Dallas needed to figure out how she fit into his life when this was all over.

Chapter Fifteen

Kate made a few calls to check on work and then spent the balance of the morning playing with her son. She had always believed that she needed work to keep her busy, to feel fulfilled, and was surprised to realize that being with Jackson was enough.

Maybe once she got her donor base full, she'd consider cutting back to working half-time. She couldn't imagine stopping altogether. Being a mother was incredibly rewarding, but feeding people filled another part of her heart.

The one thing she'd realized when she'd cashed out of her start-up was that wearing the best clothes or paying two hundred dollars to have her hair colored and cut did nothing to refill the well. Did she enjoy looking good? Of course. She still thought it was important to feel great in what she wore and how she took care of herself. But she'd figured out that she could still look pretty amazing with just the right color sweater. And a ponytail and pair of sweats were all she needed to impress the little man she was holding. Jackson didn't even care if her socks matched, which some days they probably didn't since he'd come into her life.

Her work at the kitchen was important. It felt good to make sure people were fed, to know she was making a difference for others on a most basic level.

Then there were other feelings she was having a harder time getting under control, feelings for Dallas O'Brien.

The rich cowboy was smart, handsome and successful. And he did things to her body that no man before him had come close to achieving.

It was more than great sex with Dallas. There was a closeness she felt with him that she'd never experienced with anyone else.

And yet a nagging question persisted. What did she really know about him?

Like what was his favorite color? Was he a lazy Sunday morning person or did he get up early and go out for a jog? When did he have time to work out between running the ranch and taking care of his business in New Mexico? A body like his said he must put in serious time at the gym. Heck, she didn't even know his favorite meal, dessert or alcoholic beverage.

All the little details about each other that added up to true intimacy were missing.

The one thing she knew for certain was that if she was in trouble, then he was the guy she wanted standing beside her. Dallas O'Brien had her back. And he was capable of handling himself in every situation.

Kate placed Jackson on his belly on the blanket

Dallas had spread out on the wood floor. The few toys Janis had brought were keeping her son entertained.

And she wondered how long she could keep him safe like this.

The reality of their situation hit fast and hard, like lightning on a sunny day. They were in hiding in a near stranger's house. Her mind argued that she and Dallas couldn't possibly be strangers anymore, but she pushed logic aside.

She focused on her boy, shuddering at the thought someone could want to take him from her. Rather than give in to that fear, she sipped her coffee.

There were so many facts and theories rolling around in her head. If what they'd talked about earlier was true, then she had to consider the possibility that Jackson's father was a criminal. She wouldn't love her son any less either way, but that would complicate their lives, given that this criminal seemed intent on finding his son.

If he found Jackson, and Jackson turned out to be his, she wouldn't have to worry about courts and judges, because this guy could take Jackson and make a run out of the country. He'd eluded law enforcement so far.

Kate's chest squeezed as she thought about the possibilities.

There was another option. Dallas could be Jackson's biological father. That thought didn't startle her as much as it probably should.

"Don't do that to yourself." Dallas's voice startled her out of the dark place she'd gone.

"You scared me," she said, avoiding the topic.

"Sorry. The deputy and sketch artist are on their

way here." He sauntered across the room toward the kitchen with his coffee mug in hand and Kate couldn't help but admire his athletic grace. She also thought about what he looked like naked and that sent a different kind of shiver down her back.

"Don't get tied up with what-ifs," Dallas said, pouring a fresh cup of coffee. He held up the pot. "Want more?"

She shook her head.

"It's hard." She looked at Jackson. He was such a happy baby and her heart hurt at the thought of him being taken away, let alone never seeing him again.

"My mother used to tell me that it was her job to worry," Dallas said.

"Then I'm overqualified," Kate quipped.

He smiled and it was like a hundred candles lit up inside her.

"It would be impossible not to worry under the circumstances," he conceded. "And I think it comes with the territory of parenting."

She locked on to his gaze. "I can't lose him."

"If I have anything to say about it, you won't." The sincerity in his voice soothed her more than she should allow, because nothing about their current situation said that Dallas could protect them forever.

There was a comfort in being with him that she'd never known with anyone else. "How's work? I can't help but feel we're keeping you from your own life," she said, trying to redirect her thoughts.

Dallas eyed her for a minute before he spoke. "It's

no trouble. I have everything covered here and in New Mexico."

"I appreciate all you're doing for us," she said, stiffening her back. "In case I haven't told you that lately."

"Don't do that. Don't bring up a wall between us." Hurt registered in his dark eyes.

"I'm sorry. I just don't know how to deal with this," she said, her gaze focused on the patch of floor in front of her. Feeling a sudden chill, she rubbed her arms.

"How about we take it one day at a time," he suggested. He covered well, but she detected a note of disappointment in his voice.

The last thing Kate wanted to do was hurt the one man helping her. The emotions she felt for Dallas confused her, and even though it made no sense, they felt far more dangerous than anything else they faced.

"I don't know if I can do that," she admitted.

"Will you at least tell me why not?"

"I'm scared."

"THEN LET'S NOT overthink whatever's happening between us," Dallas said, moving to her and then kissing her forehead.

She smiled up at him, which wasn't the same as agreement, and his heart stuttered.

His cell phone buzzed. He fished it out of his pocket and answered, deciding the two of them needed to have a sit-down when this mess was all over to talk about a future. Dallas had no idea what that meant exactly, but he wanted Kate and Jackson in his life.

After saying a few "uh-huh"s into the phone, he ended the call.

"Doc's here," he said, moving to the front door.

He opened it before she could knock. Dallas was ready to get an answer to at least one of his questions.

After introductions were made, he asked, "What do you need from me to get the ball rolling?"

Dr. McConnell smiled, winked and set down her bag. "A swab on the inside of your cheek should do the trick."

Kate brought Jackson over, sat on the couch and then put him on her lap for easier access. She dropped his toy at least three times before the doctor managed to obtain his swab.

"How long before you'll get the results?" Dallas asked, mostly wanting to ease Kate's concern.

"I'll walk this into the lab myself as soon as I leave here," Dr. McConnell said as she secured the samples. "So I should have news tomorrow around this time."

Kate's eyes grew wide and then she refocused on her son. Dallas could almost feel the panic welling inside her.

"Thank you for taking care of this personally," he said, standing to offer a handshake.

"You're not getting away that easily," Dr. McConnell said, pulling him in for a hug. She and his mother had been close friends. "I said it before, but I'm sorry about your folks. I miss my friends every day."

"Same here," Dallas said, appreciating the sentiment. "There's something I need to tell you before you go."

She looked up at him.

"It'll be in the news soon enough, even though Tommy is doing his level best to suppress the story, and I told my brothers this morning," Dallas said. "I thought you should know before everyone else."

"What is it, Dallas?"

"The toxicology results came back with a suspicious substance, cyanide. Mother and Pop were poisoned," he said.

It looked as though the doctor needed a minute to let that information sink in.

"That would explain your father's heart attack. He was in excellent physical condition and I couldn't shake the feeling that something was off about him having a heart attack while driving." Dr. McConnell touched his arm and drew in a deep breath. "I'm so sorry."

"Me, too."

"Why? How?" Her voice was soft. Tears streamed down her face. "They were such good people. I can't imagine anyone wanting to hurt your parents. Is there any chance the substance was accidentally ingested?"

"That's the question of the day." Dallas brought her in for another hug. "No matter what, I pledge to get to the bottom of this. If someone killed my parents, then I won't rest until they pay for what they did."

"I'd like to have the poison expert at my hospital take a look at the report. Give another opinion." Dr. McConnell wiped away her tears and straightened her rounded shoulders.

"Any additional eyes we can get on the case, the

better," Dallas said. "Any help you can give is much appreciated."

"This happened the day after the art auction," she said. "So they were around a lot of people that night and the next day."

"If they were murdered, we'll find the SOB," he said, his mind already clicking through possibilities. He'd have Tommy request all the pictures taken that night so he could figure out exactly who had attended the party. The guest list would be easy enough to locate and there'd be dozens of others—waiters, bartenders and cooks.

There was a professional photographer hired for the party, as well as Harper Smith from the society page of the local newspaper.

"I can't think of one person who would want to hurt your parents," Dr. McConnell said, still in disbelief.

"Me, either," Dallas stated.

She took a breath, pursed her lips and nodded. "If I can be of any help, you know my number."

"I won't hesitate," Dallas said.

She hugged him again before taking up her bag and saying goodbye to Kate. Stopped at the door, she shifted her gaze from Kate to Dallas. "I hope everything works out the way it's supposed to."

Dallas saw the doctor out, then turned to Kate. "Are you doing okay?"

Her shoulders sagged and sadness was written in the lines of her face. "I didn't know about your parents."

"I just found out yesterday. I'm still trying to process the news."

"From Tommy?" Kate seemed hurt that he hadn't shared the information with her sooner.

Dallas moved to her side and sat down next to her, ignoring the heat where his thigh pressed against hers. "The only reason I didn't bring it up last night was because there was so much else going on."

"It's okay, Dallas. You don't have to tell me anything," she said, trying to mask her pain and put on a brave face.

"I'd planned to tell you, but with everything else happening I was trying to process the news myself and then tell my brothers. I overloaded last night, and being with you was the only thing keeping me sane."

He leaned forward and pressed his forehead to hers. "I just hope you can understand."

She didn't say anything right away. She just breathed.

"I do," she murmured at last, and Dallas finally exhaled.

The deputy and sketch artist stopped by next. It took Dallas only fifteen minutes with the artist for him to capture the image in Dallas's mind. He thanked them before walking them both out.

For the next hour, Dallas played with Jackson on the floor alongside Kate. He sensed that her nerves were on edge.

"I wasn't expecting to feel this stressed about the test," she finally admitted.

"One phone call is all it takes to make it go away, if you don't want this to go any further," Dallas said.

"Between you and some random criminal being Jackson's father, I'm hoping it's you," she said.

"That's quite an endorsement," he responded, and he couldn't help but laugh despite all the heaviness inside him.

Kate joined him, a much-needed release of nervous tension for both of them, despite the tragic circumstances.

"Well, if I have to have a child out there, this little guy isn't a bad one to have," Dallas said. "You hungry?"

"Starving," she said. "I need to feed Jackson and put him down for a nap first."

"What sounds good?" Dallas asked, ignoring her comment. He might not be able to take care of Jackson on his own, but he could order lunch.

"A hamburger and fries," she said, making a little mewling sound.

Dallas remembered hearing a similar one earlier that morning while they'd made love. He cracked a smile, thinking how much he'd like to hear it again.

EARLY THE NEXT MORNING, the door to the guest room opened a crack. Kate pushed up to a sitting position, careful not to wake Jackson.

"Thought you'd want to know that Stacy's going home this morning," he said in a whisper.

"That's great news," Kate said. "Or maybe not. I'm worried about her being home alone."

"I'm sending Reece to stay with her just until this case is resolved," he said, and then his expression sobered. "I got a text from Tommy that Seaver has been picked up and is being brought into the station. From what I've been told, he's not real happy about it. Janis is on her way over to stay with the baby. I'll put on a pot of coffee."

Kate kissed her son, got dressed and met Dallas in the kitchen.

He walked up to her, gaze locked on hers, cradled her neck with his right hand and pressed a kiss to her lips.

"There," he said, after pulling back. "That's a better way to start the day."

"I couldn't agree more," she said, smiling. "I missed you last night."

He kissed the corners of her mouth as a soft knock sounded at the door.

"I'll get the coffee." Kate had already noticed the travel mugs on the counter.

Dallas opened the door for Janis.

"Is my baby sleeping?" she asked.

"Yes. But probably not for much longer." Kate filled mugs and brought them with her into the living room.

"Then I'll read quietly. Is he in the guest room?"

Dallas nodded as he took his mug from Kate. "Ready?"

"Let's do this," she said.

"We'll take my brother's Jeep. Colin drove it over this morning for us," Dallas said.

He had a big family. She'd met Tyler so far. She wanted to get to know the others, too.

As she said goodbye to her son and hauled herself into the Jeep, Kate wondered what it must've been like growing up in such a large family. It had been only she and Carter as children. Maybe that was why his recent closeness with their mother seemed like such a betrayal.

Dust kicked up on the road, which was barely visible in the predawn light.

"We're going to exit on the east side of the ranch, near Colin's place. He's similar in height and build, so I'm hoping no one will recognize me. You might want to get in the backseat and lie on your side until we clear the area safely."

Kate unbuckled her seat belt and climbed into the rear. "Tell me when to duck."

Chapter Sixteen

The ride to the sheriff's office went off without a hitch. Dallas's plan to throw off whoever might be watching by switching vehicles seemed to be working, and Kate finally breathed a sigh of relief when they pulled into the parking lot.

Facing Seaver had her nerves on edge, knowing he was somehow involved if not completely behind the abduction attempt.

Tommy met them as soon as they walked through the door. "He's confessed to everything," he said.

"What?" Kate could hardly believe what she was hearing.

"We're making arrangements for Seaver to turn state's evidence against Raphael Manuel," the lawman added, ushering them into his office. "Manuel was Susan's boyfriend. We connected him using the sketch you gave us yesterday.

"The man you identified is a known criminal who's wanted for murder in New Mexico and Texas. And Seaver confessed that he happens to be the father of Susan's child."

Kate's head spun as she tried to wrap her mind around the information coming at her at what felt like a hundred miles an hour. It occurred to her that while Dallas was in the clear, her son's situation still hung in the balance. Susan and this man could be Jackson's parents.

"You know this for certain?" Dallas asked.

"One hundred percent," his friend declared. "There's no way you fathered Susan's child."

The paternity-test results would prove that, but Dallas was relieved not to have to wait. "What about Susan?"

"Found out from the marshal who will handle Seaver that she is safe and tucked far away until the trial," Tommy said. "She broke off her relationship with Manuel after she caught him engaging in criminal activity, and made a desperate call to you. The Feds have been building a case ever since. With her and Seaver's testimony, Manuel will go away for a long time."

"How is Seaver involved?" Dallas asked.

"Manuel had his henchmen kidnap babies, but he learned from Harold Matthews that some of the adoptions were kept off the books at Safe Haven. Manuel tracked several to Seaver and threatened to kill the lawyer's family if he didn't help locate his son."

"And he had worked with me and Jackson," Kate said quietly.

Both men nodded.

"Which accounts for the change in MO," Dallas said.

"Seaver is deathly afraid of guns and he didn't want to take the chance that someone would get killed. The assignment was to take the babies and test them, not hurt them or their mothers," Tommy explained.

"So, Seaver arranged Jackson's abduction," Dallas said.

"And admitted to setting up Allen to throw us off the trail," Tommy stated.

"Which almost worked," Kate mused.

"Where's Manuel?" Dallas asked.

"We don't know. The marshal is processing a warrant right now so they can pick him up."

"They have to locate him first," Dallas said.

Tommy's cell buzzed. "Hold on. I need to take this."

Dallas's arms were around Kate, and for the first time in a long time, she felt a glimmer of hope.

And then Tommy looked at her with an apologetic expression. Her stomach dropped.

"Manuel must've followed Seaver's trail to your brother. Carter has been abducted."

"What?" Kate's heart sank. This could not be happening. She'd spoken to him just yesterday. Carter had to be fine.

The only thing keeping her upright was Dallas's arms around her. Her head spun and she could barely hear the quiet reassurances he whispered in her ear.

"We have to find him," she said, her knees almost giving out.

"They want Jackson," Dallas said, holding her tight. "They won't hurt Carter." His words wrapped around her, kept her from succumbing to the absolute panic threatening to take her under.

She gasped. "My phone. What if Carter tried to call? I have to get to my phone."

"Where is it?" Dallas asked.

"In the diaper bag at the ranch." Hold on. She could check her messages from anywhere.

Dallas must've realized what she was thinking, because he made a move for his own cell. "Try this."

She put the call on speaker.

Carter's voice boomed into the room. "Kate, don't do anything rash. He wants Jackson."

A male voice she didn't recognize urged Carter to tell the truth.

Her brother hesitated. "He says he'll kill me if you don't deliver Jackson to one of his men."

The line went dead.

The automatic message system indicated that the call had come in at four o'clock that morning.

"Can you trace it?" Kate asked Tommy.

"We'll do our best. Manuel most likely has a program to scramble his signal, though," the lawman conceded.

"They're somewhere local," Dallas said. "Manuel would have brought Carter here."

"What makes you so sure?" Tommy asked.

"This guy is desperate to find his son and he's narrowed his search down to this area. I'm sure Morton told him about the other local adoptions," Dallas said. "A man who goes to these lengths to find his boy would want to be right here."

Tommy nodded. "Good point. I'll check in with local motels."

Dallas held his hand up. "I might already know where he'll be."

"Morton's house." Kate gasped. "Stacy."

"Reece is with her. He's very good at his job. She'll be fine," Dallas said, his thumbs moving on the keyboard of his phone. "I just asked him to call me."

Kate immediately realized that Dallas wouldn't want Reece's cell tones to give him away, or he would have phoned the security agent himself.

Her heart pounded against her ribs.

Dallas pointed toward the landline. "Call your mother. Tell her to get out of the house and not come back until we say it's safe."

Kate did, unsure what kind of reception she'd get.

Her mother picked up on the first ring.

"Mom, it's Kate. I need you to listen carefully. Go next door and stay there until I call."

Her mother must have grasped the panic in Kate's tone because she stuttered an agreement. "What is it, Kate? What's going on?" she finally asked.

"I need you to go now. I'll explain later."

"All right," she said tentatively. "I'll wait next door until I hear from you."

"Tell Dad to be careful, too. He should stay at the office until I give the all clear."

"I'm worried. Are you and the baby okay?" It was the first time her mother had asked about Jackson.

"We're good, Mom. I'll explain everything when I can. Just go, and be careful, okay?" Tears streamed down Kate's face. She and her mother had had their difficulties, but she couldn't stand to think of anything awful happening to her.

"I will. I love you, Kate. And I'm sorry. If anything happens to me I need you to know that."

"Me, too, Mom. And I love you." Kate held in a sob, promising herself that she'd stay strong. "Call my cell when you get to the neighbor's and leave a message. Let me know you got there safely."

Kate's cell was at the ranch, but she could check the message when she retrieved it or call voice mail again using Dallas's cell.

"Okay. Take care of yourself." Her mother paused. "And give Jackson a kiss from Grandma."

Kate had wanted to hear those words from her mother for months. She promised she would do as asked, then ended the call.

Thankfully, her parents were safe. At least for now.

Dallas was urging her toward the exit as soon as she hung up.

"Any chance I can talk you out of walking through that door?" Tommy asked.

Dallas stopped at the jamb and turned.

"I didn't think so," his friend said. "Okay, fine. But we're going in with my tactical unit."

"I'm dropping Kate off at the ranch first," Dallas stated.

"They might hurt her brother if they don't see her." Tommy looked from Dallas to Kate.

"You can't take me back there. Not when my brother needs me," she declared.

Dallas's jaw clenched and every muscle in his body

was obviously strung tight. "They're going to want to see a baby."

Tommy called down the hall and a deputy showed up a few seconds later cradling something in his arms.

The plastic baby looked real from a distance. Kate took it from the deputy. "He sees me with this and he'll assume it's Jackson."

"I won't use you as bait," Dallas muttered.

"Neither will I, but I want her in the car nearby," Tommy said, before she could argue.

"We brought Colin's Jeep. I'll let my brothers know what's going on," Dallas said.

"This one needs to stay quiet," Tommy said. "There's no one I trust more than your family, but we're taking enough of a risk as it is."

Tommy called in his unit. "Kate will be in the Jeep with Dallas, here." He pointed to a spot on the Google map he'd pulled up on his computer screen. "We'll come in from around the sides while she makes contact. Our perp will be watching the front and back doors, so we're looking at side windows."

Kate glanced at Dallas, not bothering to hide her panic. "We have to get there before Stacy and Reece do."

"I know." But the expression in Dallas's eyes said it was probably already too late.

Very little was said between Dallas and Kate on the ride over. He had agreed to give Tommy's men a ten-minute head start, which wasn't much time.

Kate regretted having this go down on such a quiet suburban street. It was afternoon, but thankfully a weekend, and she hoped the cold and nearness to the holiday would keep everyone inside.

The sun peeked out from battleship-gray clouds as they approached.

"That's Reece's car," Dallas said. "But this is good. If they surprised him then we'll have someone on the inside. If I know Reece, he's already planning an escape route, and he'll keep Stacy safe."

"She's been through so much already," Kate said under her breath, hating that so much bad could strike such a good person all at once. Stacy must be terrified.

Kate cradled the pretend baby in her arms, making sure anyone watching could see. The look of panic on her face was real.

Dallas eased down the quiet road and then parked across the street from Morton's house, just as they'd planned.

The porch light flickered on and off a couple of times.

"They're signaling," Dallas said.

"What do we do now?" Kate asked.

"We wait."

But they didn't have to sit for long. There was a loud boom inside the house and smoke billowed out one of the windows.

"Stacy's in there," Kate said, her hand already on the door release.

Dallas stopped her. "We have to let Tommy do his job."

"We can't just sit here," she argued.

Dallas's door opened just then and the barrel of a gun was pressed to the back of his head.

The noise inside the house, the smoke, must have been meant to be a distraction while Manuel grabbed his son.

"I'll take that baby," a male voice said, and it had to be Manuel, based on the sketch Dallas had provided.

Kate pulled the plastic baby to her chest to shield its face from the man. If he got a good look, he'd shoot. "I'll come with you."

She made a move toward the door handle, and at the same time, Dallas jerked the guy's arm in front of him, pinning it against the steering wheel. A shot sounded and Kate's heart lurched.

"Run, Kate," Dallas cried, wrestling the gun out of Manuel's hand.

Dallas must've been putting a ton of pressure on the guy's arm, based on the look on his face.

Kate bolted. She ran straight to the house, flung open the door and shouted, "He's out front!"

Another crack of gunfire sent her stomach swirling. *Dallas.*

Tommy ran out the door toward her.

By the time the two of them reached Dallas, he had Manuel facedown and was sitting on his back while twisting his right arm behind him.

The criminal was spewing curse words.

Tommy dropped his knee into Manuel's back as he wrangled with flex-cuffs. Kate frantically searched for the gun and noticed, as Dallas turned, that he had blood on his stomach.

"Dallas," she cried with a shocked sob.

His gaze followed hers and he pressed his hand against his abdomen.

Tommy was already calling for an ambulance as Dallas lost consciousness. He slumped over onto his side as Kate dropped to her knees, unaware that she was still clutching the plastic doll.

It took ten minutes for the EMTs to arrive. Kate was vaguely aware of Stacy and Reece comforting her.

Reece drove her to the hospital behind the ambulance in his SUV. Being told that the kidnappers had been arrested did nothing to settle Kate's nerves, not while Dallas was in trouble.

She could see the gurney Dallas was on as it rolled into the emergency entrance. She asked Reece to stop, bolted out of the SUV and rushed forward.

One of the EMTs turned around. "Are you Kate Williams?"

Her heart clutched. "Yes."

"Good. Will you come see this guy? He hasn't stopped talking about you since he opened his eyes in the ambulance."

Kate nodded, tears streaming down her cheeks as she ran toward Dallas.

She had never been so happy as when he looked at her and said, "We did it. Jackson's safe."

"I love you!" It was all she could manage to say before he squeezed her hand and was wheeled away.

"TEST RESULTS ARE IN," Dallas said as he entered the room, his hand fisted around something that Kate couldn't readily make out.

"You shouldn't be out of bed," she fussed. "The doctor won't be happy when she hears about this."

He'd been a trying patient at best since Dr. McConnell agreed to let him recuperate at home.

"Well, if you aren't the least bit curious, then I'll head back to our room," he said, turning.

"Dallas O'Brien, you better stop where you are," Kate muttered.

He did. "Good to know you have that 'mom voice' perfected," he teased. "We already knew I wasn't Jackson's biological father," he continued. "Manuel is."

"Which means he's Susan's child," Kate said. "What if she wants him back now that this is all over?"

"She doesn't," Dallas said. "Said he would remind her too much of her mistakes. All she ever wanted was for him to be brought up in Bluff by a loving family. He's your son and Susan has no intention of trying to change that."

Relief flooded Kate hearing those words. The child of her heart was hers to keep.

"I heard you on the phone earlier with your mother," Dallas said.

"She's making a real effort," Kate said, beaming up at him. "Once you're well, I'd like to invite her and Dad over for dinner."

"I think that's a great idea," he said. "And what about Carter?"

"It'll be tough to drag him away from his company, but I'm determined to spend more time with family."

"About that." Dallas kissed Kate as he struggled

to bend forward. He set a small package next to her. "Christmas is a couple of months away."

"The doctor said to take it easy," she warned.

"And what's my punishment if I don't?" He winked.

"An even longer wait before we resume any more adult-only playtime," she teased.

Dallas laughed it off and grunted as he managed to sit down next to her. He made a face at Jackson, who cooed in response, causing her heart to swell.

Kate stared at the roughly two-by-two-inch Tiffany Blue Box beside her.

She opened her mouth to speak, but was hushed by Dallas.

"I know what you're thinking. You don't want to rush, because you think we need to get to know each other better," he said. "I disagree, because I know everything I need to know about you. I intend to spend the rest of our lives together bringing up this boy, our boy. I don't need a test to prove he's my son. He's yours and that's good enough for me."

Tears welled in Kate's eyes. More than anything, she wanted to say yes. Everything in her heart said this was right. "So before you say anything, here's the deal. I love you, Kate. I want to spend the rest of my life with you and Jackson. And that's all I need you to know for now. Sometime before the end of next year, I plan to ask a very important question, but the only thing I'm asking today is…will a year be enough time for you to feel like you really know me?"

"Yes." Happy tears streamed down her cheeks.

"Then hold on to that box as a promise from me,"

Dallas said. "When you finally do feel like you know me well enough, I want the three of us to be a family. I love you, Kate. And I want you to be my wife."

All Kate could do in answer was kiss the man she loved.

* * * * *

USA TODAY *bestselling author*
Barb Han's new miniseries,
CATTLEMEN CRIME CLUB,
is just getting started.
Look for DELIVERING JUSTICE *next month*
wherever Harlequin Intrigue books are sold!

THE MONTANA HAMILTONS *series*
by B.J. Daniels goes on.
Turn the page for a sneak peek at INTO DUST...

CHAPTER ONE

THE CEMETERY SEEMED unusually quiet. Jack Durand paused on the narrow walkway to glance toward the Houston skyline. He never came to Houston without stopping by his mother's grave. He liked to think of his mother here in this beautiful, peaceful place. And he always brought flowers. Today he'd brought her favorite: daisies.

He breathed in the sweet scent of freshly mown lawn as he moved through shafts of sunlight fingering their way down through the huge oak trees. Long shadows fell across the path, offering a breath of cooler air. Fortunately, the summer day wasn't hot and the walk felt good after the long drive in from the ranch.

The silent gravestones and statues gleamed in the sun. His favorites were the angels. He liked the idea of all the angels here watching over his mother, he thought, as he passed the small lake ringed with trees and followed the wide bend of Braes Bayou situated along one side of the property. A flock of ducks took flight, flapping wildly and sending water droplets into the air.

He'd taken the long way because he needed to relax. He knew it was silly, but he didn't want to visit his mother upset. He'd promised her on her deathbed that he would try harder to get along with his father.

Ahead, he saw movement near his mother's grave and slowed. A man wearing a dark suit stood next to the angel statue that watched over her final resting place. The man wasn't looking at the grave or the angel. Instead, he appeared to simply be waiting impatiently. As he turned...

With a start, Jack recognized his father.

He thought he had to be mistaken at first. Tom Durand had made a point of telling him he would be in Los Angeles the next few days. Had his father's plans changed? Surely he would have no reason to lie about it.

Until recently, that his father might have lied would never have occurred to him. But things had been strained between them since Jack had told him he wouldn't be taking over the family business.

It wasn't just seeing his father here when he should have been in Los Angeles. It was seeing him in this cemetery. He knew for a fact that his father hadn't been here since the funeral.

"I don't like cemeteries," he'd told his son when Jack had asked why he didn't visit his dead wife. "Anyway, what's the point? She's gone."

Jack felt close to his mother near her grave. "It's a sign of respect."

His father had shaken his head, clearly displeased with the conversation. "We all mourn in our own ways. I like to remember your mother my own way, so lay off, okay?"

So why the change of heart? Not that Jack wasn't glad to see it. He knew that his parents had loved each other. Kate Durand had been sweet and loving, the perfect match for Tom, who was a distant workaholic.

Jack was debating joining him or leaving him to have this time alone with his wife, when he saw another man approaching his father. He quickly stepped behind a monument. Jack was far enough away that he didn't recognize the man right away. But while he couldn't see the man's face clearly from this distance, he recognized the man's limp.

Jack had seen him coming out of the family import/export business office one night after hours. He'd asked his father about him and been told Ed Urdahl worked on the docks.

Now he frowned as he considered why either of the men was here. His father hadn't looked at his wife's grave even once. Instead he seemed to be in the middle of an intense conversation with Ed. The conversation ended abruptly when his father reached into his jacket pocket and pulled out a thick envelope and handed it to the man.

He watched in astonishment as Ed pulled a wad of money from the envelope and proceeded to count it. Even from where he stood, Jack could tell that the gesture irritated his father. Tom Durand expected everyone to take what he said or did as the gospel.

Ed finished counting the money, put it back in the envelope and stuffed it into his jacket pocket. His father seemed to be giving Ed orders. Then looking around as if worried they might have been seen, Tom Durand turned and walked away toward an exit on the other side of the cemetery—the one farthest from the reception building. He didn't even give a backward glance to his wife's grave. Nor had he left any flowers for her. Clearly, his reason for being here had nothing to do with Kate Durand.

Jack was too stunned to move for a moment. What had that exchange been about? Nothing legal, he thought. A hard knot formed in his stomach. What was his father involved in?

He noticed that Ed was heading in an entirely different direction. Impulsively, he began to follow him, worrying about what his father had paid the man to do.

Ed headed for a dark green car parked in the lot near where Jack himself had parked earlier. Jack dropped the daisies, exited the cemetery yards behind him and headed to his ranch pickup. Once behind the wheel, he followed as Ed left the cemetery.

Staying a few cars back, he tailed the man, all the time trying to convince himself that there was a rational explanation for the strange meeting in the cemetery or his father giving this man so much money. But it just didn't wash. His father hadn't been there to visit his dead wife. So what was Tom Durand up to?

Jack realized that Ed was headed for an older part of Houston that had been gentrified in recent years. A row of brownstones ran along a street shaded in trees.

Small cafes and quaint shops were interspersed with the brownstones. Because it was late afternoon, the street wasn't busy.

Ed pulled over, parked and cut his engine. Jack turned into a space a few cars back, noticing that Ed still hadn't gotten out.

Had he spotted the tail? Jack waited, half expecting Ed to emerge and come stalking toward his truck. And what? Beat him up? Call his father?

So far all Ed had done from what Jack could tell was sit and watch a brownstone across the street.

Jack continued to observe the green car, wondering how long he was going to sit here waiting for something to happen. This was crazy. He had no idea what had transpired at the cemetery. While the transaction had looked suspicious, maybe his father had really been visiting his mother's grave and told Ed to meet him there so he could pay him money he owed him. But for what that required such a large amount of cash? And why in the cemetery?

Even as Jack thought it, he still didn't believe what he'd seen was innocent. He couldn't shake the feeling that his father had hired the man for some kind of job that involved whoever lived in that brownstone across the street.

He glanced at the time. Earlier, when he'd decided to stop by the cemetery, he knew he'd be cutting it close to meet his appointment back at the ranch. He prided himself on his punctuality. But if he kept sitting here, he would miss his meeting.

Jack reached for his cell phone. The least he could

do was call and reschedule. But before he could key in the number, the door of the brownstone opened and a young woman with long blond hair came out.

As she started down the street in the opposite direction, Ed got out of his car. Jack watched him make a quick call on his cell phone as he began to follow the woman.

CHAPTER TWO

THE BLONDE HAD the look of a rich girl, from her long coiffed hair to her stylish short skirt and crisp white top to the pale blue sweater lazily draped over one arm. Hypnotized by the sexy swish of her skirt, Jack couldn't miss the glint of silver jewelry at her slim wrist or the name-brand bag she carried.

Jack grabbed the gun he kept in his glove box and climbed out of his truck. The blonde took a quick call on her cell phone as she walked. She quickened her steps, pocketing her phone. Was she meeting someone and running late? A date?

As she turned down another narrow street, he saw Ed on the opposite side of the street on his phone again. Telling someone…what?

He felt his anxiety rise as Ed ended his call and put away his phone as he crossed the street. Jack took off after the two. He tucked the gun into the waist of his jeans. He had no idea what was going on, but all his instincts told him the blonde, whoever she was, was in danger.

As he reached the corner, he saw that Ed was now

only yards behind the woman, his limp even more pronounced. The narrow alley-like street was empty of people and businesses. The neighborhood rejuvenation hadn't reached this street yet. There was dirt and debris along the front of the vacant buildings. So where was the woman going?

Jack could hear the blonde's heels making a *tap, tap, tap* sound as she hurried along. Ed's work boots made no sound as he gained on the woman.

As Ed increased his steps, he pulled out what looked like a white cloth from a plastic bag in his pocket. Discarding the bag, he suddenly rushed down the deserted street toward the woman.

Jack raced after him. Ed had reached the woman, looping one big strong arm around her from behind and lifting her off her feet. Her blue sweater fell to the ground along with her purse as she struggled.

Ed was fighting to get the cloth over her mouth and nose. The blonde was frantically moving her head back and forth and kicking her legs and arms wildly. Some of her kicks were connecting. Ed let out several cries of pain as well as a litany of curses as she managed to knock the cloth from his hand.

After setting her feet on the ground, Ed grabbed a handful of her hair and jerked her head back. Cocking his other fist, he reared back as if to slug her.

Running up, Jack pulled the gun, and hit the man with the stock of his handgun.

Ed released his hold on the woman's hair, stumbled and fell to his knees as she staggered back from him, clearly shaken. Her gaze met his as Jack heard a vehicle roaring toward them from another street. Unless he missed his guess, it was cohorts of Ed's.

As a van came careening around the corner, Jack cried "Come on!" to the blonde. She stood a few feet away looking too stunned and confused to move. He quickly stepped to her, grabbed her hand and, giving her only enough time to pick up her purse from the ground, pulled her down the narrow alley.

Behind them, the van came to a screeching stop. Jack looked back to see two men in the front of the vehicle. One jumped out to help Ed, who was holding the blonde's sweater to his bleeding head.

Jack tugged on her arm and she began to run with him again. They rounded a corner, then another one. He thought he heard the sound of the van's engine a block over and wanted to keep running, but he could tell she wasn't up to it. He dragged her into an inset open doorway to let her catch her breath.

They were both breathing hard. He could see that she was still scared, but the shock seemed to be wearing off. She eyed him as if having second thoughts about letting a complete stranger lead her down this dark alley.

"I'm not going to hurt you," he said. "I'm trying to protect you from those men who tried to abduct you."

She nodded, but didn't look entirely convinced. "Who are you?"

"Jack. My name is Jack Durand. I saw that man following you," he said. "I didn't think, I just ran up behind him and hit him." It was close enough to the truth. "Who are *you*?"

"Cassidy Hamilton." No Texas accent. Nor did the name ring any bells. So what had they wanted with this young woman?

"Any idea who those guys were or why they were after you?"

She looked away, swallowed, then shook her head. "Do you think they're gone?"

"I don't think so." After he'd seen that wad of money his father had given Ed, he didn't think the men would be giving up. "I suspect they are now looking for both of us." When he'd looked back earlier, he'd thought Ed or one of the other men had seen him. He'd spent enough time at his father's warehouse that most of the dockworkers knew who he was.

But why would his father want this woman abducted? It made no sense and yet it was the only logical conclusion he could draw given what he'd witnessed at the cemetery.

"Let's wait a little bit. Do you live around here?"

"I was staying with a friend."

"I don't think you should go back there. That man has been following you for several blocks."

She nodded and hugged herself, looking scared. He figured a lot of what had almost happened hadn't yet registered. Either that or what had almost happened didn't come as a complete surprise to her. Which made him even more curious why his father would want to abduct this woman.

ED URDAHL COULDN'T believe his luck. He'd picked a street that he knew wouldn't have anyone on it this time of the day. On top of that, the girl had been in her own little world. She hadn't been paying any attention to him as he'd moved up directly behind her.

The plan had been simple. Grab her, toss her into the van that would come speeding up at the perfect time and make a clean, quick getaway so no one would be the wiser.

It should have gone down without any trouble.

He'd been so intent on the woman in front of him, though, that he hadn't heard the man come up behind him until it was too late. Even if someone had intervened, Ed had been pretty sure he could handle it. He'd been a wrestler and boxer growing up. Few men were stupid enough to take him on.

The last thing he'd expected was to be smacked in the back of the head by some do-gooder. What had he been hit with anyway? Something hard and cold. A gun? The blow had knocked him senseless and the next thing he'd known he was on the sidewalk bleeding. As he'd heard the van engine roaring in his direction, he'd fought to keep from blacking out as whoever had blindsided him had gotten away with the blonde.

"What happened?" his brother Alec demanded now. Ed leaned against the van wall in the back, his head hurting like hell. "I thought you had it all worked out."

"How the hell do I know?" He was still bleeding like a stuck pig. "Just get out of here. *Drive!*" he yelled at the driver, Nick, a dockworker he'd used before for less-than-legal jobs. "Circle the block until I can think of what to do."

Ed caught a whiff of the blonde's perfume and realized he was holding her sweater to his bleeding skull. He took another sniff of it. *Nice.* He tried to remember exactly what had transpired. It had all happened so fast. "Did you see who hit me?" he asked.

"I saw a man and a woman going down the alley," Alec said. "I thought you said she'd be alone?"

That's what he had thought. It had all been set up in a way that should have gone off like clockwork. So where had whoever hit him come from? "So neither of you got a look at the guy?"

Nick cleared his throat. "I thought at first that he was working *with* you."

"Why would you think that?" Ed demanded, his head hurting too much to put up with such stupid remarks. "The son of a bitch coldcocked me with something."

"A gun. It was a gun," Alec said. "I saw the light catch on the metal when he tucked it back into his pants."

"He was carrying a gun?" Ed sat up, his gaze going to Nick. "Is that why you thought he was part of the plan?"

"No, I didn't see the gun," Nick said. "I just assumed he was in on it because of who he was."

Ed pressed the sweet-smelling sweater to his head and tried not to erupt. "Are you going to make me guess? Or are you frigging going to tell me who was he?"

"Jack Durand."

"What?" Ed couldn't believe his ears. What were the chances that Tom Durand's son would show up on

this particular street? Unless his father had sent him? That made no sense. *Why pay me if he sent his son?*

"You're sure it was Jack?"

"Swear on my mother's grave," Nick said as he drove in wider circles. "I saw him clear as a bell. He turned in the alley to look back. It was Jack, all right."

"Go back to that alley," Ed ordered. Was this Tom's backup plan in case Ed failed? Or was this all part of Tom's real plan? Either way, it appeared Jack Durand had the girl.

CASSIDY LOOKED AS if she might make a run for it at any moment. That would be a huge mistake on her part. But Jack could tell that she was now pretty sure she shouldn't be trusting him. He wasn't sure how much longer he could keep her here. She reached for her phone, but he laid a hand on her arm.

"That's the van coming back," he said quietly. At the sound of the engine growing nearer, he signaled her not to make a sound as he pulled her deeper into the darkness of the doorway recess. The van drove slowly up the alley. He'd feared they would come back. That's why he'd been hesitant to move from their hiding place.

Jack held his breath as he watched the blonde, afraid she might do something crazy like decide to take her chances and run. He wouldn't have blamed her. For all she knew, he could have been in on the abduction and was holding her here until the men in the van came back for her.

The driver of the van braked next to the open doorway. The engine sat idling. Jack waited for the sound of a door opening. He'd put the gun into the back waistband of his jeans before he'd grabbed the blonde, thinking the gun might frighten her. As much as he wanted to pull it now, he talked himself out of it.

At least for the moment. He didn't want to get involved in any gunplay—especially with the young woman here. He'd started carrying the gun when he'd worked for his father and had to take the day's proceeds to a bank drop late at night. It was a habit he'd gotten used to even after he'd quit. Probably because of the type of people who worked with his father.

After what seemed like an interminable length of time, the van driver pulled away.

Jack let out the breath he'd been holding. "Come on. I'll see that you get someplace safe where you can call the police," he said and held out his hand.

She hesitated before she took it. They moved through the dark shadows of the alley to the next street. The sky above them had turned a deep silver in the evening light. It was still hot, little air in the tight, narrow street.

He realized that wherever Cassidy Hamilton had been headed, she hadn't planned to return until much later—thus the sweater. He wanted to question her, but now wasn't the time.

At the edge of the buildings, Jack peered down the street. He didn't see the van or Ed's green car. But he also didn't think they had gone far. Wouldn't they expect her to call the police? The area would soon be crawling with cop cars. So what would Ed do?

A few blocks from the deserted area where they'd met, they reached a more commercial section. The street was growing busier as people got off work. Restaurants began opening for the evening meal as boutiques and shops closed. Jack spotted a small bar with just enough patrons that he thought they could blend in.

"Let's go in here," he said. "I don't know about you, but I could use a drink. You should be able to make a call from here. Once I know you're safe…"

They took a table at the back away from the television over the bar. He removed his Stetson and put it on the seat next to him. When Cassidy wasn't looking, he removed the .45 from the waistband of his jeans and slid it under the hat.

"What do you want to drink?" he asked as the waitress approached.

"White wine," she said and plucked nervously at the torn corner of her blouse. Other than the torn blouse, she looked fine physically. But emotionally, he wasn't sure how much of a toll this would take on her over the long haul. That was if Ed didn't find her.

"I'll have whiskey," he said, waving the waitress off. He had no idea what he was going to do now. He told himself he just needed a jolt of alcohol. He'd been playing this by ear since seeing his father and Ed at the cemetery.

Now he debated what he was going to do with this woman given the little he knew. The last thing he wanted, though, was to get involved with the police. He was sure Ed and his men had seen him, probably recognized him. Once his father found out that it had been his son who'd saved the blonde…

The waitress put two drinks in front of them and left. He watched the blonde take a sip. She'd said her name was Cassidy Hamilton. She'd also said she didn't know why anyone would want to abduct her off the street, but he suspected that wasn't true.

"So is your old man rich or something?" he asked and took a gulp of the whiskey.

She took a sip of her wine as if stalling, her gaze lowered. He got his first really good look at her. She was a knockout. When she lifted her eyes finally, he thought he might drown in all that blue.

"I only ask because I'm trying to understand why those men were after you." She could be a famous model or even an actress. He didn't follow pop culture, hardly ever watched television and hadn't been to the movies in ages. All he knew was, at the very least, she'd grown up with money. "If you're famous or something, I apologize for not knowing."

SPECIAL EXCERPT FROM

⊞ HARLEQUIN®

I N T R I G U E

*When attorney Natalie Drummond loses pieces of her
memory and starts experiencing hallucinations, no one
but B&C Investigations detective Clint Hayes believes
the danger she's sensing is real.*

*Read on for a sneak preview of
DARK WHISPERS,
the first book in USA TODAY bestselling author
Debra Webb's chilling new spin-off series
FACES OF EVIL.*

Natalie's car suddenly swerved. Tension snapped through
Clint. She barreled off the road and into the lot of a
supermarket, crashing broadside into a parked car.

His pulse hammering, Clint made the turn and skidded
to a stop next to her car. He jumped out and rushed to her.
Thank God no one was in the other vehicle. Natalie sat
upright behind the steering wheel. The deflated air bag
sagged in front of her. The injuries she may have sustained
from the air bag deploying ticked off in his brain.

He tried to open the door but it was locked. He banged
on the window. "Natalie! Are you all right?"

She turned and stared up at him. Her face was flushed
red, abrasions already darkening on her skin. His heart
rammed mercilessly against his sternum as she slowly hit
the unlock button. He yanked the door open and crouched
down to get a closer look at her.

"Are you hurt?" he demanded.

"I'm not sure." She took a deep breath as if she'd only just remembered to breathe. "I don't understand what happened. I was driving along and the air bag suddenly burst from the steering wheel." She reached for the wheel and then drew back, uncertain what to do with her hands. "I don't understand," she repeated.

"I'm calling for help." Clint made the call to 9-1-1 and then he called his friend Lieutenant Chet Harper. Every instinct cautioned Clint that Natalie was wrong about not being able to trust herself.

There was someone else—someone very close to her—she shouldn't trust. He intended to keep her safe until he identified that threat.

Don't miss DARK WHISPERS
by USA TODAY bestselling author Debra Webb,
available in September 2016 wherever
Harlequin® Intrigue books and ebooks are sold.

www.Harlequin.com

HIEXP0816

Turn your love of reading into rewards you'll love with

Harlequin My Rewards

Join for FREE today at
www.HarlequinMyRewards.com

Earn **FREE BOOKS** of your choice.

Experience **EXCLUSIVE OFFERS** and contests.

Enjoy **BOOK RECOMMENDATIONS**
selected just for you.

PLUS! Sign up now
and get **500** points
right away!

Earn
FREE
REWARDS
HarlequinMyRewards.com
Join
Today!

MYR16R

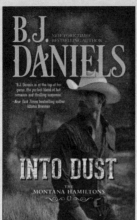

EXCLUSIVE
Limited Time Offer

$1.⁰⁰ OFF

New York Times Bestselling Author

B.J. DANIELS

He's meant to protect her, but what is
this cowboy keeping from her about the
danger she's facing?

INTO DUST

Available July 26, 2016.
Pick up your copy today!

HQN™

$7.99 U.S./$9.99 CAN.

$1.⁰⁰ OFF the purchase price of INTO DUST by B.J. Daniels.

Offer valid from July 26, 2016 to August 31, 2016.
Redeemable at participating retail outlets. Not redeemable at Barnes & Noble.
Limit one coupon per purchase. Valid in the U.S.A. and Canada only.

52613799

5 65373 00076 2 (8100)0 12169

® and ™ are trademarks owned and used by the trademark owner and/or its licensee.

PHCOUPBJD0816

THE WORLD IS BETTER WITH

Romance

Harlequin has everything from contemporary, passionate and heartwarming to suspenseful and inspirational stories.

Whatever your mood, we have a romance just for you!

Connect with us to find your next great read, special offers and more.

f /HarlequinBooks

🐦 @HarlequinBooks

www.HarlequinBlog.com

www.Harlequin.com/Newsletters

(H) HARLEQUIN®

A *Romance* FOR EVERY MOOD™

www.Harlequin.com

SERIESHALOAD2015